Leave a Crooked Path

Simone Paradis Hanson

SHADOWLIGHT
- press -

First Printing 2016

ISBN 978-0-692-74557-1 Shadowlight Press LLC
simonehanson.wordpress.com

Book cover design by Steve Plummer spdesign@hargray.com
Author photo by Maura Roberts Photography

Ordering information: Available from Ingram Spark

For My Mother

Acknowledgments

It takes a great deal of effort and time to write a first novel. It's too much to accomplish alone. Happily, I had the amazing support of the world's best writing group to prop me up and keep me going. All my heartfelt thanks to Sam Moffitt, Ashley Owens, Kevin Ramirez, Jaager Good and Brent Lambert.

Thank you to my husband, John, for his unwavering support, and to my three boys Adrian, Duncan and Jack. I appreciate you keeping the noise down in the man-cave so I could get my work done. That means a lot.

Laura Rosen and Kristin Schoonover are extraordinary friends. Thank you for being my first readers and for your enthusiastic support and encouragement.

Thank you to Erin Farwell for her editing expertise, as well as her enthusiasm in jumping into the agony of starting a small press publishing company. I wasn't really sure you'd say yes, but I'm glad you did. This has been fun.

And finally, thank you, Readers, for taking a chance on this book.

CHAPTER One

O ur next door neighbor, Mrs. Bergeron, suffered from Jumping Frenchman of Maine Syndrome. According to my father, this condition is also known as Exaggerated Startle Response, which is basically an attack of the nerves characterized by loud shouting and flailing. If a person with this disorder gets a sudden scare, they'll yell out whatever word happens to be on their mind at the exact moment they were startled. They also jerk their arms around wildly, a little like a marionette whose handler is having a coronary. Mrs. Bergeron had an especially amusing tendency to react to sudden, sharp commands by doing exactly what she was told.

Every year on Halloween, my father would dress up completely in black and ring her doorbell. He'd leer in at her and yell as loud as he could, "Put your hands up!" She'd fling the bowl of candy she was holding straight up over her head and shout out something like, "Miracle Whip!" I swear, you could go a whole year without laughing and that one night would make up for it.

You couldn't be faulted for wondering how a woman like that ever finds a husband, but then when you saw Mr. Bergeron, it all made sense. He was getting old and bald, only had eight fingers total, and walked with a limp. He lost his fingers in two separate lawn mower accidents and broke his leg when he accidentally limbed the tree branch he was standing on. The resulting disfigurements made him a hero to all the little kids in the neighborhood. There was something thrilling about inching close enough to get a good look at his hands, to see the stump of the lost fingers jutting out between the whole ones, the ends cut smooth, the skin shiny and red.

On Saturday afternoons during the summer, Mr. Bergeron would come outside and sit on a lawn chair in his driveway, pop open a can of beer and light a cigarette. The snap of the beer tab was like a siren call. He'd balance a big plastic bowl filled with candy on his knees and wave at whatever kids were outside playing. "Here you go kids," he'd say. "Have at it." He was like Jesus with the bread and fish, the way he always had enough, no matter how many of us there were. The little kids, the ones who were still flagrantly selfish, would beg for two handfuls, or ask him how much they could have. "Take what you want," he'd say. "I got plenty." And he'd hold the bowl out, nodding his head and telling us to make sure to dig down to the bottom, sometimes the chocolate pieces settled.

Mr. Bergeron was my father's boss down at the iron works, the big shipyard on the river where they built battleships that were half a mile long, enormous skyscrapers laid on their sides. On those sunny afternoons, when he'd be handing out his candy, he'd make it a point to tell me and my sister that our father was the best welder in the neighborhood. And then he'd add, "Of course, he's the only welder in the neighborhood!" and that would make him laugh so hard, he could barely hold onto the bowl.

It never got old for him. Grace would laugh at the joke, her high pitched fake laugh, but I always found it a little insulting. Welders are the ones who melt lead with a blow torch, making sure all the seams on the ship are fused shut, keeping the hulls tightly sealed against the ocean. They keep the ships afloat. It seemed pretty important to me, but it's hard to hold a grudge against someone when he's holding a big bowl of candy in his open palms and saying "Here, take all you like." But I limited myself to a couple of Charleston Chews, one to eat right away, even if it was a warm day and the chocolate melted all over my fingers, the other to put in the freezer and eat later that same night, after smashing it on the counter and eating the splintered pieces one at a time.

It was hot out, the day Mr. Bergeron lost his third finger. Even though I was fourteen and about to start high school, I have to admit it was a little disappointing to hear the beer can crack open only to turn around and see him set the can down on the front steps and go into the garage. He emerged a few minutes later with the lawn mower and a gas can. I was lying out on a beach towel next to my friend Celeste, the two of us trying to burnish our pale skin with baby oil and iodine. It was early August, three weeks till the end of summer. Our life goal at that moment was to make sure we had a tan. To keep our minds off the boredom of just laying there, we listened to a small transistor radio that played a steady stream of static behind the music, and every three songs we turned over, like chickens on a rotisserie. It was a good method, it gave us a nice even burn all the way around.

Celeste and I had been friends as far back as our memories extended. Her mother once told us we were Siamese twins who had been surgically separated at birth. For the longest time, we believed it. It bothered us, that someone had cut us apart with a scalpel. To make up for it, we'd sometimes braid our hair together which forced us to stay within inches of each other. "This is what we would have been like," we'd whisper to each other, and we'd walk around like that until our hair came undone.

"We should go to the beach," Celeste said. "I'm roasting." We had just rolled over onto our backs and our eyes were closed against the piercing sun. "Want to ride bikes to the Pond?"

An airplane began to pass low overhead and momentarily blocked the sun. It was a carrier, one of the really big planes that can carry a fleet of tanks. It was heading in the direction of the naval base, which was a few miles from our neighborhood. There was a training station there, and planes were constantly passing over us, everything from tiny high speed jets that left sound in their wake, to these big, heavy machines that seemed to hardly move at all. I always worried about the big planes, that they'd stop and drop out of the sky when they were right over my house. I had to wait for it to pass before I could answer, it drowned out all other noise.

"I can't," I told her, once the gray plane was miles past and we could hear each other again. "My uncle's coming over for dinner. I have to make a dessert."

"Well that stinks," she said, sitting up and staring at me. I had to shade my eyes so I could see her. She had these really big eyes, almost like a cartoon character, though I never would have said that to her face. She was kind of proud of her eyes. Even squinting in the bright sun, they were penetrating, and I knew she was waiting for an invitation, though she knew dinner with my uncle wasn't a walk in the park. He came on a little strong. I tried to ignore her by turning to look toward Mr. Bergeron. He was pouring oil and gasoline into a Tupperware pitcher and then slowly twirling the container around to mix it up. He paused to take a puff on the cigarette that hung between his lips and then poured the mixture into the gas tank. It took him two or three pulls on the cord to get the motor running and for a second it looked as though he wouldn't be able to start it. Then the motor came alive with a screech so loud and unexpected, he jumped back.

The lawnmower threw wisps of hot smoke into the air that floated in random directions like lost phantoms. He waved the smoke out of the way, took another long drag from his cigarette and started mowing. It had been at least a month since the last time he'd mown the lawn and the grass had grown pretty tall. I watched him for a while, kind of mesmerized by the way the mower passed through the tall grass and over the clover that had cropped up all over the yard. It was magical almost, all those sharp blades of grass and pink heads laid out in front of the mower, disappearing completely between the two front wheels, leaving behind an empty carpet of green.

"What are you making for dessert?" Celeste asked me, yelling as loud as she could over the sound of the mower, but the engine cut out halfway through her sentence and made her voice ring loudly in the sudden silence. The stillness was noticeable to us, but Mr. Bergeron kept on pushing the mower a few more steps before he seemed to realize that it had stopped working and the grass wasn't getting any shorter. Then it took him another few seconds to figure out what to do, which was pretty much what all men did when something broke. He tapped it, kicked the tires a few times and pulled a few levers, none of which helped. He scratched his head for a moment, and then cocked his head to one side in the international sign of confusion. He finally pushed the mower over onto its side, exposing the blades, and knelt down to get a good look.

Now, here's why you don't drink on a Saturday afternoon and then get the idea that you want to mow the lawn: when a rock lands in the blades of the mower, you will realize that the rock needs to be dislodged, but you will forget to actually turn off the mower. When you pull the rock out, the blades will start up again, fast and immediate, and your hand will be in the way.

The loud screech started up in an instant, but we couldn't tell if the sound we heard was coming from the whine of the mower or Mr. Bergeron, who was rocking back and forth on the ground, one hand clutching the other against his chest, hollering for his wife. A circle of blood spread its way evenly and quickly across the front of his shirt like a big bulls eye. Mrs. Bergeron hurried out, drying her hands on a dish towel.

"Throw me a towel!" he screamed.

"Duncan Hines!" she screamed back, hurling the towel into the air in his general direction and turning to run back in the house.

When Mrs. Bergeron disappeared, Celeste and I were alone, the only two witnesses. It was a frightening moment, we didn't know what to do about carnage. Mercifully, the screaming acted as an alarm and before we could ask ourselves what in the world we were supposed to do, the neighborhood converged. Screen doors slammed all around us and someone was yelling, "Call an ambulance. For God's sake, call an ambulance, he's done it again!"

You would have thought everyone had been standing right by their doors waiting for some catastrophe to strike, that's how fast the neighbors came streaming out of their houses. Miraculously freed prison inmates couldn't have hit the street faster. Celeste and I continued to sit on our towels, watching the mob gather on the Bergeron's front yard. We turned the radio down so we could hear better, but Mr. Gerard, the neighborhood's self-appointed president, was the only one we could hear clearly and he was just repeating over and over that an ambulance would arrive any minute and for everyone to just remain calm. Everyone else was standing around being calm.

Thirteen families lived on our street, and pretty much every household was represented at the accident site, which was typical, since no one in the neighborhood put a lot of stock in gossip. Second hand information was risky, some vital detail could be lost forever. We all thought it was best to get a story straight from the source whenever possible, so not many would pass up the opportunity to hurry over and see what was going on. Mr. Dion, the old man who lived across the street from me, was even buttoning up his pants as he hurried over.

Then again, Celeste was always telling me I underestimated people, so maybe it was something more. This was Maine after all. A place that sometimes felt more like an extension of Canada than part of New England, where dumb Frenchman jokes were tolerated since it's ok to make fun of yourself. It could be a rough place to live, but a place where no one passed a stalled car or stray dog. It was the kind of place where the truckers, hauling lumber on their forty foot flatbeds, rode the middle of the highway when the weather turned bad so the idiots and flatlanders were forced to slow down. It was a place to be endured, and thanks to people like long haul truckers and neighbors, we didn't have to do it alone.

So on this day, the neighbors would eventually do what they did best. They would stand around for a while, getting their bearings, and then they would hurl themselves into action. There would be bandages, a shot of brandy, steady hands to pick Mr. Bergeron up off the ground and settle him into his lawn chair, words of comfort and later, food. I could see it in his face, even with baby oil smearing my vision, he knew he was going to be all right. Maimed again, but he would heal.

Someone in the crowd procured a roll of bandages and wrapped it carefully around Mr. Bergeron's hand. With that done, there was nothing left to do but take turns patting the injured man on the shoulder, make sure he was sipping his beer, and wait for the ambulance. It arrived a minute later, lights twirling and siren screaming, which Mr. Gerard took as his cue to start shouting that the ambulance had arrived.

"Here she comes! Get out of the way folks, let's help get the man inside this meat wagon!" After a minute or two, it left again with Mr. Bergeron inside and his wife following behind in their Buick. "OK folks, show's over," Mr. Gerard yelled as everyone started heading home. He waved his arms in all directions like he was dispersing an especially unruly crowd.

"Well, that was fun," Celeste said. We sat with our legs stretched out, arms behind our backs to prop us up. After a few minutes, only the kids were left outside, and they made their way over to us, jumbled together like a single being. "Did you see that?" they asked us all at once, like they shared one voice as well as one body, a strange, echoing creature. My sister was the first to disengage and she sat down next to me. "You should have seen it Claire, it was so gross."

"I saw it the last time," I told her. "Once is enough for me. Plus we had a pretty good view from here."

Celeste's little brothers, Peter and Paul, were the only ones not jumping around like maniacs. They took blood seriously. "So much blood," one of them said. "I hope he won't bleed to death before they get him stitched."

"It's not like he got shot," I told them. "Mr. Bergeron will be all right." But they shook their heads anyway, granite faced.

"Hey," Celeste called out. Her voice was loud and commanding, so all the little kids turned to look at her. "I'll give a quarter to whoever finds a severed finger. No lie, a real quarter."

Celeste could be disgusting at times. A couple of the younger ones looked like they were going to throw up and then they all scattered, heading back to whatever they were doing before. I got up and walked across the lawn to the Bergeron's yard to switch off the engine to the lawn mower. It was still softly whining, like some troubled pet that was sorry for the horror it had caused. I was careful as I stepped near the machine since I was barefoot and there was a real possibility a finger was hidden in the overgrown grass. I didn't go out of my way to search for it since I wouldn't have known what to do if I found it. It was so long ago, that day, long before fingers could be reattached, back in a time when people had to live with what they'd done.

As I reached for the handle of the mower, I noticed a leaf dancing on the edge of the switch. At first I thought it was a butterfly or one of those huge dusty moths that flies around in the summer and that it was caught somehow, but it was only a dry leaf that was stuck in a thin strand of cobweb, pitching in a wind that was not quite strong enough to free it. I reached over and cut the engine, silencing it. For a brief moment, it felt like I'd just killed something.

CHAPTER Two

My mother was the one person in the neighborhood who had not attended the disaster. She could hear it, she said, and that was enough. The three of us - my father, Grace and I, sat around the kitchen filling her in on the details. "I was right there," Grace told her, "at the end of the driveway, when suddenly I heard him swear really loud. Want to know what he said?" She was just about to turn eight and for some reason had the impression that eight was a swearing age. "No, we do not want to know what he said," my mother told her. "Go find something to do," she said, her look just sharp enough to let Grace know better than to continue.

"Aw, c'mon," my father said to her, "you have to admit, it's pretty funny, considering. Two lawnmowers, one snow blower? Someone could write a book about it."

My mother turned her back on him and busied herself in the kitchen. She did not have a sense of humor about Mr. Bergeron. She didn't have much of a sense of humor at all, come to think of it. My father believed this was the direct result of her being German. Apparently they have no sense of humor, the Germans. I could sort of see it. Trust me, it was really hard to make her laugh. We tried. She'd get a slight kick out of maybe one in five jokes, she didn't get puns at all, and you could forget about making a play on words. Take, for example, her German friend, Seymour Katz. Whenever she mentioned his name, we went weak.

"I don't understand this," she'd fume, "no one laughed at him in Germany!"

And then there was her friend Isabelle who, like my mother, married an American serviceman. Frederick Ringling. Whenever she started talking about her, my father would hold his fist up to his ear and say, "Hello? Hello?" Or sometimes he'd yell, "Would someone get the door?" She'd shake her head and say something like idiotisch or dumkopf, which we could all understand and it would just make us laugh more. And then there was her maiden name, Bumgardner. That one practically sent us to the hospital.

But she was who she was, my mother, cast into place a like a bronze statue, and our jokes ricocheted off her. She was impenetrable. So many pieces come together to make a person what they are, and where these pieces come from, that's what makes the difference. My mother was born in Germany, and she was a teenager during the war. She grew up in Dresden and when the Allied forces bombed the city, she saw people she knew, family and friends, vaporized right in front of her, swallowed by huge flash fires that went off all over the city, a nightmare of flames that seemed to spring from cracks in the earth, terrible and unexpected. The firestorm that lasted three days and destroyed the center of her city was the keystone to her character, the piece to which every other part of her connected. Only my mother and her father survived, her older sister and mother extinguished, she would tell us, like a candle pinched between two fingers, that easily and quickly. There was a special kind of beauty to this bedtime story and it never failed to send Grace flying to my bed at night, clinging tightly to my arm until she fell asleep, victim of a real life Grimm's fairy tale. I heard my father ask one night if it was really appropriate for us to hear that. "They need to know," she'd answered. "Bad things happen everywhere, they should be prepared."

Most people, when they survive the unendurable, accept it as a miracle, a divine gift for the chosen few. But my mother wasn't the type to see her survival as any miracle. She took it more as a warning, one she felt compelled to hand down like a precious family heirloom.

So all this is to say my mother didn't have it in her to appreciate Mr. Bergeron's antics. She felt bad for him, I could see it in her face whenever we'd talk about Mr. Bergeron's latest accident, reenacting the scenes over and over. She didn't think joking around was the appropriate response to someone being so seriously and permanently injured. Even if it was his own fault. At the news of this latest tragedy, she drummed her fingers against each other like she did whenever she was nervous or upset about something. "We have a blueberry pie in the freezer." She didn't direct her voice to anyone in particular. "Watch for their car, Claire. When they get home, bring it over to them. I know Emile likes blueberry pie." I said I would. I was looking forward to it. I thought I might get a glimpse of Mr. Bergeron's hand and wind up with a good story.

The whole time Mr. Bergeron was being persecuted by his lawn mower, my mother had been in the kitchen. Dinner was simmering on the stove, a heavy beef stew, just what everyone wanted to eat on a hot summer day. It was the only thing she knew how to make, besides waffles. Normally my father made supper, but since he'd worked the graveyard shift, he'd been sleeping all day. The fact that my father did the cooking in our house was a blessing we would have taken for granted if it weren't for the few occasions my mother had to fill in for him. My mother threw chunks of meat and vegetables in a stock pot with water and a bouillon cube, ignored it all day and called it a meal. My father, on the other hand, was a creator.

He scoffed at Betty Crocker, thought she was a fraud. "She gets paid for coming up with baked mayonnaise casseroles? What is this world coming to?" he'd yell when he came across one of her recipes in the Ladies Home Journal. At family or neighborhood gatherings, someone always proudly brought over a molded dessert made of gelatin and small fruit chunks. A culinary atrocity, according to my father. "It's like eating prehistoric beetles suspended in amber! Call that a dessert? I call it a travesty! Travesty. Claire, do you know what that word means?"

He wouldn't wait for an answer. Which disappointed me, since I knew words better than I knew food.

But I was learning to appreciate my lot in life. Unlike the sorry public, we didn't eat supper, we dined. We dined on things I couldn't pronounce correctly, like puttanesca and bouillabaisse, rich salty dishes that we ate in silence because we didn't notice time was passing. He changed the color of rice from white to gold by adding threads of saffron, so expensive he hid the tiny bottles in the back of the cupboard so my mother would never find them. Give him a stick of butter, and he could make a sauce out of dirt.

But on this day, it was up to my mother and me to get a meal on the table, and it was standard fare. Substandard might be more accurate. I took a box of pudding mix out of the cupboard, something my father tried hard to ignore, but couldn't. He shook his head slightly in distress. "Next week," he said, "I'm going to show you how we make a custard. It's time you learned, I can't have you cooking out of a box forever."

I did my best with the dessert, I even thought to add a teaspoon of almond flavoring to the chocolate pudding, because Uncle Romeo was coming for dinner and I didn't like to see him disappointed. If my uncle got hit by a bus, he'd stay alive for my father's cooking. Tonight was going to be a great disappointment to him and I was sorry about it. We didn't like to let him down, since his life had been a timeline of disappointment, beginning with a rough childhood and culminating in his job as a gravedigger. Okay, not a gravedigger, we just said that because it sounded impressive. He was the head of maintenance down at the city cemetery.

Even though we all loved him, Grace really loved him. She would have loved him even if he wasn't our uncle. She was taken with him and the feeling was mutual. Grace was Uncle Romeo's favorite person. Or favorite living person. Don't ask me why, but he had an affinity for dead people. He loved his job at the cemetery, tending to the grave sites as though he worked for those who lay beneath them, not the living relatives who paid for the tiny lots of land or visited regularly. He told me once he didn't like how the dead could only be forgotten and so he kept them alive the best he could. The cemetery was so beautiful, so green and pulsing with flowers and hundreds of sea rose bushes, that over the years he'd turned the place into the closest thing the city had to a park. At some point it even became a state landmark, something Uncle Romeo took direct credit for. Appropriately, in my opinion.

Once it was deemed a landmark, every fifth grade class at the Nathaniel Hawthorne Elementary School had to go on an annual field trip as part of the Local History unit to view, first hand, the hundred-year-old burial sites of our founding fathers. Uncle Romeo took a personal interest and appointed himself guide of every one of them. Which worked out well, since Uncle Romeo was a born storyteller and he was in his element at the cemetery. All those dead people who couldn't contradict him and all those little kids who hung on his every word? It was perfect.

The only world famous person actually buried in his cemetery was Robert Tristram Coffin, the poet, which was fine, but with all the famous people from Maine, Uncle Romeo was a little disappointed that not more of them died here. But, no matter. He'd wave his arm toward the worn, weather-faded gravestones off in the distance that no one could read anyway, and start talking about Henry Wadsworth Longfellow, Nathaniel Hawthorne, and Harriet Beecher Stowe, who started the Civil War! All by herself! And his favorite, Joshua Chamberlain. "Won the Civil War, yes he did!" Uncle Romeo would shout. "And don't let anybody tell you different," he'd add, with a dark glance at our teachers, who looked at each other and then up at the sky. At the end of my own fifth grade field trip, I overheard Mrs. Mariner whisper to the other teachers that it was time to go back and unteach everything he'd said.

"Oh, I know it," said Mrs. Belanger, the oldest of the fifth grade teachers and the one who had been on the most field trips, "but he is awful cute."

I suppose by some standards my uncle could be considered cute, the way elderly spinsters think cats are cute. He had thick chaotic hair, which was pure white for as long as I'd known him. He had watery blue eyes that made him look like he was always on the verge of tears. And he did have a tragic past, and I think we mostly loved him because of that.

Uncle Romeo had been a hockey player in high school, and a good one. The best goalie in the high school league, according to my father. And when he was a senior, word got out that the Bruins were sending a scout up from Boston. "They were coming for Romeo, everyone knew it. That's how good he was," my father would tell us.

And for Guy LaMare. The two of them, fierce opponents, were the league stand-outs, Romeo for his fearless defense of the goal, and LaMare for his sheer skill and legendary strength. Together, they were the Paul Bunyons of youth hockey.

But in the third game of his final season, Romeo stopped one goal that he should have let pass. The way my father always told it, they could have made a movie out of it, the way he blocked every shot with the skill of a pro, playing way beyond his years, way beyond anyone else on the ice. Except for his only real opponent, Guy LaMare, who took his final shot like he was firing a cannon.

The crowd almost brought the roof down when he failed to score, but went dead silent when they noticed their goalie wasn't moving. Romeo had taken the puck right between the eyes and it took him down. He was out for several seconds before making his shaken way out of the arena, to a standing ovation. My father always told the story like he didn't think we'd really believe him, or that we couldn't possibly understand the roar of the crowd that was like thunder, so loud that he clung to his mother, thinking the trembling bleachers were going to cave in.

The next week, a scout from Boston really did come up. Romeo wasn't on the ice because his eyes were still swollen shut and he hadn't gotten his balance back and so the Bruins lost what may have been the best goalie they ever had.

By the time Uncle Romeo was back on his feet, his hair had turned white and his eyes weren't good. Such were the pieces that made him what he was, a rough man with a loud voice, but fragile at the same time.

When he came over that night, Grace was ready, jumping in front of him with her arms outstretched, wanting to be picked up, even though she was just about eight years old and really, it was time for her to move on and start acting her age. But she was little and adorable, so Uncle Romeo said, "Grace, who set you on fire?" He launched her in the air and settled her against him. She poked two fingers against his upper lip, where he had two pinprick scars.

"How'd you get these?" she asked, same as she always did.

"Kissed a snake," he said. "Wouldn't recommend it."

My mother always said he got that scar from someone stapling his mouth shut, probably one of his wives, which was certainly believable.

We lived in a small house. I would never have noticed how low the ceilings were, or how close together the furniture was nestled if I never witnessed my father and uncle in the living room at the same time. Uncle Romeo would always sit on the couch, because Grace needed to sit next to him. My father would sit in the recliner. Once settled, it seemed all the space in the downstairs was gone. I could have perched on the edge of the recliner, but I would have been conspicuous. My mother beat me to the couch.

"Claire, can you set the table for me? I'm exhausted all of a sudden."

Sure she was. That crockpot took a lot out of a person. I was going to complain that actually making the dessert was considerably more work, but Uncle Romeo was already starting one of his stories. He was sighing and shaking his head sadly. Grace perked up and my father adjusted the lazy boy so it wasn't all the way back.

"Fine," I said.

I listened as I moved around the table, setting out plates, bowls and cups, knives and forks with paper napkins folded underneath. I settled the dishes down carefully so I wouldn't make any noise. Listening to Uncle Romeo's stories was a little like going to the movies.

He told us about a bad accident on Route One, the multi-car pile up that everyone was talking about. "Hit head-on," he said, "it was terrible. Just terrible." He rubbed his face with his hand. If he was a man who ever cried, this is what it would have looked like.

I dropped a spoon and there was a momentary silence. Not so much from the sharp noise of the spoon bouncing off the table, clanging against the porcelain plate. More from the story's omission. It was a drunk driver who had caused that accident.

Five cars. One fatality. A little girl was killed, a little three year old girl. The story started up again, Uncle Romeo's gravelly voice somehow soothing. She would be buried at the cemetery, in a plot he had spent the entire day preparing. "They say she liked roses. I planted a young shrub for her, directly behind her little gravestone. It'll be nice for her, I can guarantee you that." He spoke with conviction, because he knew being buried in his cemetery was the next best thing to actually being alive.

We sat in silence after that story, sad and uncomfortable. That's the way it went with Uncle Romeo sometimes. Dinner was ready, the table was set, but it seemed inappropriate to jump up and start eating without a short period of mourning, so we stayed where we were.

The cuckoo clock ticked audibly and I was afraid the idiot bird would pop out and start tweeting. It would have been an ignominious ending to the story, so I was glad when my father straightened out his chair. The foot rest snapped shut and he stood up. "Let's eat," he said.

"Good idea," my mother said. "We should eat before the stew gets cold."

"Stew?" Uncle Romeo phrased the word as a question, a faint hope in his eye that maybe he had misunderstood. Like I said, there was probably no one who appreciated my father's cooking more than my uncle. My father could have become an arsonist and Uncle Romeo would still have thought humanity began with his younger brother all on account of his cooking. So it was with a lot of self-pity that Uncle Romeo took his seat, a heavy sigh coming from deep in his chest that I only noticed when my mother cooked.

As the bread and butter were passed around the table, my father served the stew, heavy and brown with potatoes and carrots stained red from the beets she insisted belonged in a stew. Another atrocity my father would shake his head over. Once everyone was served, my father asked Uncle Romeo if he would do the honors, and we all bent our heads slightly as he gave grace, doing a good impersonation of someone really happy to be eating stew on a hot night.

But as it turned out, it wasn't such a bad meal after all. The heavy air that had made us feel like we lived in a swamp, finally gathered itself together and formed thick clouds that began to cover the setting sun. The sky grew dark with gray clouds and thunder began to rumble in the distance. Once the wind picked up and started blowing through the open windows, it cooled everything down.

"So Claire," my uncle said to me, "you're always so quiet. What's new with you? Staying out of trouble?"

I looked around the table, not sure how to take his question. Had somebody said something about me? Technically, I never really got into trouble. I had a great sense of how to skirt justice, and while I never went so far as to break a rule outright, I'd get pretty close. I liked to dance on the edge of a cliff.

"Well, I've been ok," I said.

"You looking forward to school starting? You going to be what?

Freshman?"

"Yup," I told him.

"You going out for any sports? You know, your father played hockey. I did, too. But your father, now there was a hockey player we could be proud of. Captain of the team, did you know that?"

Grace and I exchanged a look with my mother, who shook her head slightly at Grace when she crossed her eyes. My father didn't notice, and started talking about Uncle Romeo and what an all-star he was and then we heard the hockey-puck-between-the-eyes story again and that let me off the hook for the rest of the meal.

When supper was finished and the stories told, we sat for a while, quiet, not sure how to get back to the present. It had gotten dark in the house.

"You know, I was thinking," Uncle Romeo said. I perked up, because whenever Uncle Romeo had a thought, it usually led to something interesting.

"That branch you have hanging over the house, I don't like the look of it. It's high time we took that down, why don't we go outside and take a look?"

My father said, "Sure, we could take a look. What would that hurt?"

"I am happy to give you my professional opinion, Cap'n," Uncle Romeo said, clapping my father on the shoulder as he followed him out the door.

OK. There was no way Uncle Romeo was going to have a helpful opinion about that tree. The last time my father asked him for help, we ended up needing a new dishwasher. And that wasn't the only avoidable disaster we'd experienced. But my father would let Uncle Romeo decimate every appliance in the house because, like everyone else, he had a soft spot for him, this inexplicable need to make sure he was happy. I had to wonder, though, whether my father would really put a chainsaw in his hands and tell him it was all right to take down a tree.

But that tree branch was an issue, no doubt about it. We had a huge oak tree that grew close to the house. Whoever built our old house probably thought it would be so nice to have an oak tree growing right next to the front porch, like maybe the close proximity would turn the tree into a good friend, some type of protector. But the tree was a freak of nature. The branch that stretched across our roof was bigger than our station wagon, and a lightning strike the year before had marred it with a deep black gash. A wound that severe could only have weakened it and every time there was a strong wind that blew through the neighborhood, we could hear it creaking as though sending us a warning.

As my father and uncle stepped out into the evening air, it started raining slightly, a thin mist that preferred to hang in the air rather than fall to the ground. The street lights had come on, and the light was reflected off thin air, creating a sort of dark brightness. My mother and I cleaned up and when the two of them came back in the house, they looked damp and dreary, wearing the weather on their faces. Uncle Romeo was saying he could come over tomorrow, right after church, and the two of them together could hack it off, that he had a chainsaw just waiting for the opportunity to do some hard labor. My mother's back straightened so rigidly, I swear I heard it crack.

"Well," my father started, and my mother said, "Hold on, don't we have plans tomorrow?" The two of them started talking at the same time, years of trying to head Uncle Romeo off in another direction having allowed them to hone their telepathic skill at coming up with the same excuse at the same time.

"Yes, didn't we talk about doing something tomorrow?"

"Yes, I think we did."

"What was it again?"

"The beach? Yeah, weren't we going to the beach if the weather's good?"

"Summer's about over, why not?"

My mother looked slightly stricken, as she had just voluntarily agreed to go to the beach, a place she avoided like old people avoid leaving a tip. She would have preferred visiting a mental institution. Neither she nor Grace had much use for the beach. The sand was too hot, the water was way too cold and there was always a wind whipping the sand around, which they compared to being sandblasted. I was proud of her, of the lengths she'd go to keep Uncle Romeo off the roof.

"Well," my father summarized, just to make sure everyone was clear, "if it's wet tomorrow, we won't want to be up on the roof and if it's nice out, we'll be heading to the beach."

"All right, all right," Uncle Romeo said, "I get it, you're busy. Don't make a meal out of it."

"Join us if you want to Romeo," my father added brightly.

Uncle Romeo said he might, he'd meet us over there if he got around to it, but not to wait for him.

"Just look for the big yellow umbrella!" my mother almost shouted, trying to sound as lighthearted as my father.

We all smiled as Uncle Romeo headed toward the door, saying good night and thanking my mother for her unbelievably wonderful stew. With his hand on the door handle he said, "I've got next weekend free, if no one needs burying that is, so let me come by Saturday or Sunday, we'll take 'er down. Don't like the idea of that thing hanging so low to the house."

"Sounds good," my father said as he stood with him at the door. "Drive home safe now, it looks like it really might start up here any minute." As though voicing agreement, thunder rolled somewhere off in the distance, like an avalanche heading our way. He shut the door, making sure to snap the porch light on so Uncle Romeo could make his way down the steps to his car.

The misty particles of rain grew bigger and heavier and started to hit the ground. The wind picked up and lightening flashed, brightening the house in short bursts of static. We stood together in the living room, all eyes on the ceiling, trying to determine if the wind was strong enough to crack the branch.

"Maybe the girls should sleep on the couch tonight," my mother suggested, worry behind her eyes, her fingertips tapping against each other.

"That branch isn't so bad," my father said. "Take a lot more than a little rain to shake it loose. I didn't want Romeo up there, that's all. They'll be all right. But I am calling the Menards in the morning, have them come over some day next week and take it down."

The storm worsened overnight. The wind was so loud I heard

screaming in my sleep and a crack of thunder woke me up. It was dark in my room, the darkness so complete it felt as though everything had been inked out, except when the lightning flashed and then everything was brighter than day and I could see that my room was still there.

By morning, the storm was gone. The sun was bright, reigning over a clear sky as though nothing had happened. But a transformer had been hit, and the whole neighborhood was out of power.

CHAPTER Three

Y ou'd think we were under a nuclear attack.

This had happened years before, when I was too little to re-member, even before Grace was born. The whole neighborhood had lost power when a car slammed into a telephone pole and knocked down a transformer. I'd heard so many stories about it, I almost remembered being there myself. The neighbors had all pulled their grills to the bottom of their driveways and had a cook-out with all the meat they had stored in their freezers. It sounded like a lot of fun. So I was curious why this time the neighborhood was in a panic. But that's what French-Canadians do, I guess. They panic. At least when their food is at risk.

In a dream-like state, my parents walked down the driveway, Grace and I behind them. Our neighbors, most of them anyway, were outside in their bathrobes, milling around like the neighborhood had just been detonated.

"I bought a side of beef yesterday, can you believe that!" Mr. Gerard was yelling, his wife shaking her head in disbelief.

Everyone had a side of beef or pork in their freezers, it's another thing we did, we bought meat in bulk from a butcher, who wrapped it in crisp white paper, handwritten labels telling us what was inside. Pork sausage, bacon, ribs, steaks, hamburger, all frozen and white, stacked in freezers all over the neighborhood. And if we didn't get power back it would all defrost, begin to rot and eventually turn into carrion.

The first rule in a situation like this was to not open your freezer, in order to conserve the cold air. So once everyone had opened their freezers and counted the packages, we had a rough idea of how much food had been imperiled by the storm. As the stunned neighbors milled around the neighborhood, Mr. Gerard announced, "Well, it seems like we got plenty to go around." He still had his pajama top on but at least had taken the time to pull on a real pair of pants.

Gradually, the men all gathered in a loose circle at the end of our driveway. The only one missing was Mr. Bergeron, but we could see him standing in the front window of his house. He was getting a read on the neighborhood, I could tell. Mrs. Bergeron would report back to him after the meeting and fill him in. "Here's what we'll do," Mr. Gerard announced after a few minutes of intense debate, an undeniable tenor of pride in his voice that he was finally in charge of something important. "No one do anything right now. If the power comes back on between now and tomorrow afternoon, we should be ok. Don't open your freezers, just leave them alone, and your meat shouldn't thaw out and we'll be all set."

The crowd of neighbors moved closer, nodding in agreement, murmuring prayers that this would ultimately be the case.

"But if it doesn't come back on by late Monday, we'll have a cook-out Tuesday night. Get your charcoal ready, bring your appetites, since it sounds like we've got four thousand pounds of meat all together."

Celeste found me in the throng of children. She was already dressed, as she was up and out the door early most days. She asked what I was up to, if we had any plans.

"We're going to the beach. Want to come?"

"I can't," she said, looking down at her feet. "I can't go to the beach. I mean the ocean, I can't go to the ocean. But I could go to the pond, if you want to ride bikes to the pond." She stuttered a little, like she always did when she was nervous.

She wasn't allowed to drive with us. She said her mother made a new rule one day, for no good reason, that she wasn't allowed to drive with anyone in the neighborhood. But I knew, she wasn't allowed to drive with us. Only my family.

"My mother's coming," I said.

"Um. I still think I probably can't go. I'll ask, though. I'll ask."

There were different kinds of drinkers in our neighborhood. There were the weekend drinkers like Mr. Bergeron, relatively harmless. At least to other people. There were the clown drinkers, the ones who only drank at special occasions, like weddings and funerals, and made fools out of themselves. Then there was my father. The type who can't be trusted behind the wheel of a car. But this summer had been good. A dry summer, if you will.

"I'll ask," she said again, but I knew she wouldn't.

Once the crowd of stunned people had all wandered back inside, we headed back in, too. We made breakfast without the use of the stove, opening and closing the refrigerator as fast as possible. It's amazing how many food items you need when you're not supposed to open the fridge. I kept wanting another glass of milk and Grace kept opening the door, panicking, and forgetting what she was looking for. She must have opened the refrigerator door a thousand times and still couldn't put a complete breakfast together.

What we really should have done was clean it out. Another vestige of my mother's war torn past was her determination not to waste food, and consequently our refrigerator was stuffed with probably one hundred tiny containers of leftovers, all waiting to spoil and be thrown out. But my mother couldn't throw anything away until it had started growing hair, which it would do a lot faster now that the refrigerator was warming up. So with that to look forward to, we got ready to go.

Without electricity, we couldn't use the stove, so we didn't have the usual Sunday morning 30-30-30 special - thirty minutes to cook, thirty minutes to eat and thirty minutes to clean the bacon grease off the stove. My parents couldn't even have a cup of coffee, so we'd made it to early mass at St. Mary's.

It was the worst mass, the one all the old people went to. Even though it wasn't as crowded as the later mass, it still managed to smell worse. There was a noxious odor that moved across the pews, part mothballs, part damp tweed, and it gave me a headache. I also did not like old Father Fortin. He enjoyed smoky incense. I mean, he loved it. The thick smoke he blew around the altar was probably the reason he became a priest. And he spoke with such a thick French accent, I could never understand what he was talking about, not that I would have paid much attention anyway. And the poor old people looked confused, too, since not many of them had bothered to learn English. Altogether, it was kind of a waste of time.

But the worst part was not being able to see Father Bob, the new and improved version of Catholic clergy the church was enticing into the order. Father Bob gave the eleven o'clock mass and made Sunday mornings endurable, enjoyable even, especially when he had to step down to the first row of pews to give communion to a person in a wheelchair. I always marched the family to the front of the church if I saw a wheelchair or crutches. Today, I sat as far back as I could, away from the fumes.

The car ride to the beach was not an improvement. The road was winding, and my father drove too fast. The smell from the church still clung to me and we had to stop halfway so I could jump out of the car and throw up. I was still a little shaky by the time we parked the car, so I leaned against it and breathed, replacing the smells of the church with the rich, salt smell of the ocean air.

"Let's go," my father said. "We ought to be able to get a good spot, it's pretty early." We were always one of the last people to make it to the beach on Sundays, so we'd have to walk about a mile, picking our way between other people's beach blankets and umbrellas until we found a space big enough to fit our stuff on. It would be nice to have an open beach in front of us for once. We loaded ourselves up with all our stuff from the trunk - the cooler my father had filled before we left for church, two huge beach bags with towels and toys, a quilt, two beach chairs and the beach umbrella. We looked like camels ready for a sub-Saharan journey. We headed down the boardwalk toward the beach.

It was low tide.

"Pretty low," my father said, his words tense, "but not all the way out, and it's coming in at least." My father and I did not like it when the tide was out. Low tide left the beach scaly and littered with broken shells and tiny dead fish and crabs that had mistimed the ebbing tide. The sand turned hard and cold, no longer soft and giving under your feet. When the tide was out, the beach looked harsh and past its prime. Acres of dead, wrinkled skin. He just didn't like the look of it and neither did I.

"Oh well," he said. "Nothing we can do about it."

We got set up. Everyone had their job. Grace and I spread out the quilt, placing the cooler on one end while my mother set the chairs up on the other end to keep the quilt from blowing around. My father drove the handle of the umbrella deep into the sand; if it wasn't too windy, it would stay there without falling over, casting a circle of shade against the bright sand.

"Well, this is nice," my mother said. "It's different here when it's not so crowded."

It's true, it was nice to have an open view of the beach, at this point only dotted with a few other families, to be able to see the waves as they crept up the shore, reaching as far as they could before being sucked back down. It was a new experience for us. I mentioned that we should try to get to the beach early more often, forgetting for a moment that it would mean missing the late mass.

The sense of wonder didn't last. Without more people on the beach, we got bored. It's not fun to throw a Frisbee around if you can't kick sand all over other people, I guess. So we decided to walk down to Fort Maritime, the old granite fort that marked the end of the beach.

My father double checked the cooler to make sure no seagull could pry off the top and eat our lunch, and we headed off. It was starting to get hot, and we avoided the scorching sand by walking in the shallow water, warm from the sun. When we got tired of that, Grace and I went out to where it was deeper and ran races in waist deep water, moving slowly, screaming when we hit a patch of wavy seaweed hidden in the opaque green water. When we finally reached a turn in the coastline, the fort appeared before us, small in the distance, but gradually growing bigger as we approached, until it loomed above us.

The fort stood like a sentinel at the opening of a channel, a wide expanse of water that pulled the Kennebec River into the open ocean. It had been built by overanxious Mainers who thought they might play a bit part in the Civil War, but it seems the Confederates never actually considered attacking the coast of Maine. We got a really nice granite fort out of the deal, so that's something.

The fort was made from chiseled blocks of granite stacked on top of each other, forming thick walls that encircled a small field. The structure was two stories high, with huge openings that faced the inner grounds and small slits in the thick granite walls that faced the ocean. Gunner holes, my father said they were called. Armed soldiers could push a rifle through and shoot at enemy ships sailing past, if any ever came along. It sat atop a cluttered pile of rocks. At high tide, the rocks weren't visible and the fortress looked as if it was standing on solid ground. At low tide, the rocks emerged and made the fort appear off-balance, almost precarious, as though it could easily shift on its tentative foundation and topple, scattering the granite boulders like a cascading house of cards.

Granite spiral staircases were built into the corners, and to Grace this transformed the fort into a castle. She floated up the stairs and I followed, glad to get out of the heat. The sun cast dancing shadows against the far wall as Grace twirled around like she'd suddenly found herself in a ballroom. It never took her long to get dizzy so I watched her dance around until she stumbled. Laughing, she sat down on a ledge beneath one of the long, rectangular gunner holes, where a long-dead soldier was meant to place a knee for leverage so he could shoot at enemies of the union and not lose his balance.

"Tell the story," she demanded.

She had a favorite story, one I'd made up for her a long time ago when she was so small she could still sit on my lap. Every time we climbed the stairs to the second floor of the old fort, she wanted to hear it again. Most people get tired of things by a certain point, but Grace couldn't get enough romance in her life. Sometimes I worried about her a little, she had such a quest for romantic tragedy like she was some displaced Victorian heroine. It probably came from my mother and her stories of terror and survival. We were hardly a Dr. Seuss sort of family.

So I told Grace her story one more time, sitting next to her on the ledge beneath the gunner hole. Her blond hair was pulled back in a ponytail and stray hairs that had come loose stuck to her neck and throat, damp with sweat. She smelled like candy. She always smelled like candy, even when she was sweaty and sprayed with sea water.

A long time ago, there was a young and pretty woman.

"Did she have blond hair?"

"Yes, she did Grace."

"Was it long? Like mine?"

"Yes Grace, she looked a little like you. Are you listening?"

So anyway, she fell in love with this man, and after they married, he built her a summer house on that island.

Grace turned to look out the gunner hole, across the wide reach of the channel. A long, narrow island separated the channel from the open ocean and on the end of it, perched above a rocky ledge, sat a white house. Grace stared at this house every time she listened to the story, fixated by the sagging shape of the structure, neglected for decades. Enormous stone chimneys on either side of the house were chipping and falling away. The roof line bent like a broken back between them. The rancor of twenty winters had left its mark on the face of the house, long strips of peeling paint uncovering the bleak grayness of the bones that lay beneath, weakened but still standing, a pitiful show of delusional grandeur.

Every year the house looked darker, the sills all broken, barely able to hold up the cracked windows. I continued the tragic account of Leila, the young wife, whose handsome husband had built her a summer house on a band of pine studded land, a house meant to signify a life of wealth and with it, of the happiness it was meant to bring. But the first summer after the house was built, the husband lost everything. Leila left the house early one morning and took the path he had cleared for her that led down to the small beach that appeared like a mirage between outcroppings of rock.

She went swimming in the channel. She had taken the dog with her, but he stayed on shore. Dogs can smell danger, keenly smell things that aren't visible to us. They breathe in danger so deeply, it seeps into their blood like poison. The dog ran, legs trembling, up and down the silent beach, whimpering. He ran halfway up the path, back toward the house, but then thought better of it and ran back to Leila, howling into the wind. Maybe he thought if he called to her, she'd turn around.

The channel is no place to swim. What the dog couldn't see, the hidden thing it could only sense, was the current. It runs through the channel like something living, something with a life force strong enough to wrap itself around anything within reach and hold it close in its grip, not letting go unless it wants to. The dog knew it was there, but Leila was careless. She shouldn't have thought she could swim forever.

At some point she must have realized she was moving away from the island that held the safety of her beach, her private house. The story goes that the dog made a dash up the pathway, a half-crazed mass of frenzied barking and panic. By the time the husband made his way down to the beach, his wife had disappeared.

He left the next day. He never even packed up the house, just left everything there, as though everything was suddenly untouchable.

"That is so sad," Grace was still staring at the house, willing it back to life. My parents had joined us by this point and my father started talking about the history of the fort, wrecking the mood. Then he took out the Instamatic he always brought with him to the beach and lined us up for a picture. "One more," he said, just to make sure he got a usable print, despite the fact that we had fourteen years' worth of pictures taken at this very spot.

Then we heard screaming. At first just one voice but then two. And then shouts from more people. The four of us tried to look out the narrow slit in the wall at the same time. We couldn't see anything but slate gray water and the house sitting crooked on the shore of the island.

"I think someone's in the water," my mother said. "They're yelling for help." My mother started to tap her fingers together, her nerves coming alive as the shouting grew more frantic. We all headed for the staircase, except for Grace, who was mummified.

"C'mon Grace," I said. "What's wrong with you? Let's go. Don't you want to see what's happening down on the beach?"

"What if it's her?" My sister's voice so low I had to bend close and tell her to say it again. "What if it's Leila?"

The yelling from the beach got louder and Grace looked at me, still not moving. That's all she needed. Another image to be afraid of. I took her hand and led her back down the spiral stairs, assuring her that Leila had died a long time ago, remembering too late that I had made her up, she didn't even exist.

We caught up to my parents who had joined the growing crowd on the beach. My mother had been right, there really was someone in the water. It took just minutes to put the story together from the crowd that milled around at the water's edge, huddling together, eyes focused on a small form floating close to the middle of the channel. He was someone's fifteen year old son, one of three boys who thought it might be fun to swim across the channel to the island. The two brothers had turned back, leaving the youngest to prove himself. Now they were hysterical, screaming across the water for him to come back. They were up to their knees in the water, rolling waves rising to their waists and then falling back down. There must have been a slight undertow, because as the waves receded, the boys lost their balance

The boy's mother was easy to spot. She jumped around on the beach, yelling. From a distance, you might have thought she was a cheerleader. "Why won't someone help?" she was screaming. "Someone get him. Please!"

Her husband was trying to calm her down, telling her he had run to a rental house and called the Coast Guard, that they were on their way and everything would be all right. But she'd given herself over to panic.

It's amazing how, in a crisis situation, so few people are able to think clearly. It frankly made no sense to do anything besides wait. Even the boy's father was trying to calm everybody down, saying the Coast Guard was sending a boat out and that the first thing he ever taught his son was how to float. But that didn't stop a dozen men, including my father, from stepping into the water as they looked out toward the boy, who now seemed to be floating safely on his back.

I blame the mother, I blame her insistence that people wade into the water and get her son, her boy who shouldn't have been out there floating around in the middle of the channel to begin with, silently heading out to sea on the current. Her insistence that bordered on belligerence, making every man on the beach feel as though he had to try and help. She kept up her badgering as the men walked deeper into the cold water. Deeper and deeper until they had no choice but to swim.

Before you knew it, the channel was filling up with a bunch of fat out-of-shape dads, their arms and legs throwing tangled water into the air. Now everyone on the beach fell into that kind of quiet panic, the kind where some people crossed their fingers, others crossed their hearts, no one's eyes leaving the forms in the water except to throw a glare at the mother, who was finally silent. All sympathy for her was suddenly gone, turned away from her like a changing wind. Now we were all angry.

Even though they weren't moving with the greatest of speed, most of the men had managed to get pretty close to the kid by the time the Coast Guard finally showed up. They arrived on the scene like a happy ending, the suave hero that rolls in after everyone else has done all the work. They handily plucked the boy out of the water and then blew an announcement over the waves telling all the would-be rescuers to head back to shore immediately. No thank you, no note of appreciation in the voice that bellowed over the incoming waves. Just a dismissal. And the Coast Guard vessel, no more than a whaler, floated in the water and the crew watched as the men bobbed around as though they were waiting for a medal.

Then gradually, like a really slow school of fish, they all turned around and headed back to shore. My mother was holding Grace's hand, her other hand shading her eyes against the sun. Grace was crying, repeating over and over that she couldn't see Dad. There was good reason for that. As the men pulled themselves, dripping wet, out of the surf, we searched, but my father wasn't there. Other families crowded around us, pulling their tired, shivering fathers onto the hot sand, covering them with towels. My mother and I looked around wildly, but we couldn't see him. It was as though he had vanished. And that's when my mother started screaming.

CHAPTER Four

Situations can always be worse. But that doesn't mean it can't be bad, it all depends on who you are and what the world looks like to you. My father was in the Coast Guard vessel, blue lipped and shivering. He had swum the fastest, leaving the other fathers in his wake, and had been the only one to reach the boy, but it had exhausted him. The boy had gotten caught in the same current that had carried the imaginary Leila out to sea. I was actually a little surprised that the current was as strong as I had imagined it, and the boy really had made it about a quarter mile from shore. Because my father had been swimming the whole way instead of floating, exhaustion and hypothermia had made it hard from him to move in the water and he had been hauled into the boat along with the boy, like a wounded fish. To my father, this was mortifying. He did not like appearing weak. It was not something he ever said, it was just something that was very noticeable about him. He once dug a splinter out of his foot that was practically lodged in the bone. My mother had wanted him to go the doctor, we all had. Grace almost passed out watching him try to get to it with a pair of tweezers, but he kept saying he didn't need a doctor, it was just a splinter.

It didn't matter how seriously he might be hurt, he couldn't admit to an injury and he couldn't admit to a mistake. One day at work, he put his safety goggles on as he walked into a welding area, not before like he was supposed to. A sliver of hot metal sailed through the air at that exact moment and landed right in the soft spot under his eye. It swelled up and for weeks the burn got increasingly worse until my mother was afraid he'd lose sight in that eye. But he'd go blind before he went to a doctor. He'd take blindness over an admission that he didn't get his glasses on fast enough and that a slice of metal, melted against his skin, had done him in. He now had a small scar under his lower eyelid, a reminder of his strength every time he looked in the mirror. A reminder that he didn't need anybody.

As he stepped over the side of the boat, his knees gave way slightly, and my mother had to grab his arm until she was sure he could stand.

"What happened?" she asked one of the crew members, a young guy with a thin beard, who wasn't wearing a hat like the other men. His wispy hair blew around in the wind.

"Is he all right? Is it his heart?" She was yelling, trying to be heard over the sound of the engine.

"For Christ sake, Marie! I'm fine. Christ!" My father was hunched over and shivering, but I could still tell he was yelling. Or trying to.

The parents of the boy took their time reaching the boat, at least the mother did. She clearly was hoping her husband would get there before her; you could tell she wasn't the type to get her feet wet. The kid jumped out of the boat and his father yanked him onto the sand, where the mother threw her arms around him. She let out a wail so loud I wondered how far it would be carried on the wind before no one heard it anymore. The boy, whose name was Pete, at least had the decency to realize he had caused some trouble. He looked down at his feet as he pulled away from his mother and stumbled back to where his brothers were waiting for him. They threw him a towel and took turns punching him on the shoulder, each punch a little harder than the last, and he kept saying, "Cut it out Fembot. I didn't see you swim out that far."

The Coast Guard boat slowly slid away from the beach, heading out of sight as it passed the fort. My father was saying he was all right, he just got a cramp, that was all. He stood up straight as his feet hit the dry sand, once again becoming the tallest person on the beach. He put his arm around my shoulder and told me to stop looking so scared.

"Some hero, huh?" he said.

Grace still looked like someone had hit her with a live wire, she was pale and walked like there was a numbness coursing through her. My mother kept trying to hold my father's arm, asking him again and again whether it was his heart.

"I'm all right," he finally said. "Take more than a dunk in the ocean to kill me. I got a cramp. Just a damn cramp."

He picked up Grace and told her everything was fine. Her face was stone, as hard as the granite that had made the fort. He put his face close to hers until their noses touched, like they used to do when she was little. He told her he wouldn't put her down until she smiled. Her smile was a thin line across her face.

This was our fear, a crack in the façade. Broken pieces he couldn't fix, exposed every now and then by a mistake, by an accident or bad luck. If he couldn't keep it hidden, he'd hide it another way. He'd hide it with drinking. Of course, that only hid it from himself. He could hide the whole world from himself. Just not us.

But this was just a little setback. We could make sure it remained a small thing, needing help from the Coast Guard to return to shore. Not a major failing, he had swum halfway to the island, after all. Kind of funny, actually, if you thought about it long enough.

"Hey Dad," I yelled. "What happens when a Coast Guard cutter crosses a steelworker?"

"What?" he said.

"It founders. Get it? Founders? Like foundry?"

"Good one," he said. "I like it."

"Dad," Grace asked, "did you swamp the boat when they pulled you in?"

"Hey! What are you saying?" He lifted her high in the air again, this time over his head, and settled her down on his shoulders. Even my mother started to loosen up. On and on, all the way back up the beach. We made jokes, we laughed about it. We had to, it's what we did, we laughed until the enormity of it had shrunk down to a size we could hold in one hand and toss around.

While we'd been busy saving drowning children, the beach had been invaded by an onslaught of families, all with their own assorted beach gear, umbrellas and bedspreads. Seagulls flying overhead might have thought someone had spread out a massive quilt for them. One of those gulls was perched on our cooler like he owned it and was waiting till he was hungry to open it up and dig in.

"Who wants to eat?" my mother asked. The gull hopped off the cooler, but stayed close, stomping back and forth along the edge of our blanket, angry that we were preparing to eat his lunch. He was what we called a flourishing gull. He was fat, obviously well fed, and had an unmistakable authority, one of those seagulls who never gets attacked by the rest of the flock. He seemed pretty put out that we weren't showing him the respect he was accustomed to.

I don't remember in exactly what we did the rest of that day. But I know what we must have done, because it's what we always did and I don't remember it any other way. We would have cleaned out the cooler, emptied it of sandwiches, chips, apples and drinks. We would have tricked the seagulls into catching apple cores and then watched them start a war over something none of them even wanted. Grace and I would have built a sandcastle with a deep moat and towers for protection, watching as the waves gained strength and washed over them again and again until everything we'd built had disappeared. We would have packed up all our stuff and headed back to the parking lot, loaded down like the tourists we always made fun of. And before I stepped onto the boardwalk, I would have turned around to get a final look and I would have noticed that the tide had come all the way in, that the beach was now covered with silvery blue water, the sun's reflection glancing off the surface, scattering shards of light across the swelling waves.

It is a crushing sky.

All day the purple clouds have been dropping lower, so swollen and heavy with rain, they have trouble floating up high, where they belong. The forecast predicts rain but they haven't predicted precisely when the clouds will open up and let go of the storm they are holding.

I'm a little confused on this day because neither of my parents have gone to work, but I know it isn't a holiday because there's a steamroller heading down our street, rolling slowly in our direction as it smoothes hot tar into a new road. There is a parade atmosphere in the air, a bunch of us are lined up along the side of the road, hopping in anticipation of the steamroller reaching us and grinding its way past.

"Here it comes! Here it comes!" Celeste screams. The men who walk backwards in front of the steamroller, raking the tar to an even height, laugh at her and shake their heads at each other. They're old and they do this every day. They don't know the thrill of an enormous piece of machinery, a gliding robot, puffing steam and spitting water out its sides. We imagine all sorts of things, what it would be like to get our foot stuck under it, what if someone laid down in front of it? How cool would it be to see a watermelon splatter under two tons of unstoppable steel? Let's throw pennies in front of it, they'll be preserved in the tar, like fossils! But no, there's no time to run inside and grab a handful of loose change, we might miss the steamroller as it goes by. It passes us so slowly and yet it goes by too fast. This road won't be tarred again in our lifetimes.

My mother has taken Grace out somewhere, I didn't pay attention to where. She didn't want her outside when there was so much danger out on the street, so she left the house before the work started. My father is angry. He hasn't been able to leave the house because of the hot, slushy tar and the steamroller that is in the way. Now he stalks over to the men who are standing at the end of the street, where the road dead ends at the woods. They are going to take a break and then head back down the other side, so we'll get to see the big machine pass by one last time, smoothing the rough wet tar that has to be flattened, making one wide, even road. We test the new road with our feet, taking turns standing on it, seeing if we will sink. We don't, and of course that's because the steamroller has packed it down and we are feathers compared to its enormous weight. Apparently a car can drive on it as well, and my father comes toward us. He is using a wide stride and his hands are clenched tight. He tells me to get in the car, says for Celeste to get in the car too, since we are watching her today, her mother is sick.

We are only eight, and we can't say no, and my father is wearing such a dark face, we don't ask to please wait so we can watch the steamroller go past us for the last time. We leave the neighborhood, driving fast, and I'm too nervous to ask my father where we are going, so Celeste and I just sit quietly in the back seat, each of us looking out a different window. He drives into town and turns down the road that runs behind the grocery store, parking in a small lot outside a bar.

"C'mon, follow me," he says, and we get out and follow him up the rotted wooden steps which make a wet, spongy sound under our weight.

"Frank," the man behind the bar says, not as a greeting, not as a question. He just says the name, like it's some sort of test he has to pass in order to be a bartender, demonstrating that he knows every patron's name. It reminds me of flashcards.

It's dark inside, all the lights are hooded by heavy shades. My father tells us we can sit at the tall barstools. That they're fun, they spin around.

"What'll you have?" The bartender is old, he has hair so gray and thin, it floats like cobwebs around his head. He has white hairs that grow out of his nose and ears and when I look over at Celeste I can tell by her face that she has noticed the same thing. He ignores us.

My father orders a drink for himself and tells the man that we'll have Shirley Temples.

"Claire," he says, leaning in close to me, his hand on my back. "Want me to have him give you a couple extra maraschinos? I know you like them." He winks at me and tells the bartender not to skimp on the cherries. He is happy here and so he is not mad at us anymore.

He winks again, this time at the bartender when he brings the pink drinks to me and Celeste, both our glasses loaded with cherries. "Thanks friend," he says, but the bartender looks to the door where someone has just come in and says another man's name in the same flashcard reading voice he used when we came in. My father looks down at the bar where *his hands rest on either side of two small glasses filled with liquid gold.*

He finishes the two drinks very quickly. His hand shakes each time he carries the glass to his mouth. He asks Celeste and me if we want another drink and waves the bartender back over, but we've both hardly touched the ones we have. The bartender brings another golden drink over, he doesn't even wait for my father to order it. He drinks this one more slowly, stopping between sips to run his finger around the rim of the glass, like he is trying to get it to make a ringing sound like we do at home sometimes. When that drink is gone, he gets up slowly from the tall barstool. He tells us he'll be right back.

"Don't go anywhere, ok? I'm just going to be gone a second." His words are spoken perfectly. But very slow.

"OK."

"Just stay right there on those stools. Promise?"

We nod. I think he's just going to use the bathroom, but I hear the door shut behind us and I turn around and I can see him through the dull glass of the window. He's running across the parking lot, taking short fast steps as he keeps looking up at the sky. He looks as though he's afraid the clouds will burst open and a torrent might sweep him away.

Celeste looks at me and asks, "Where's he going?"

I tell her I don't know and she says she wants to go home, she's a little scared in this bar and she doesn't think she's really allowed to be here. But I don't know what to do. I keep turning to look out the window. I know where he has gone. There's a liquor store on the other side of the parking lot, and he has gone to buy himself a few days worth of alcohol, golden brown liquor with a crass smell, not quite bitter, not quite sweet, swirling in clear glass bottles.

We sit and wait. There is a mirror across from us, I can see pieces of us in it. I think no one else knows there is a mirror there, shelves filled with bottles are lined up across it, as though they think there is only a wall there. I can see our arms. Circles around our drinks.

When my father finally comes back in, he has two brown paper bags, one in each hand. He places them on the bar and sits back down on the stool next to me and says to the old man bartender, "How 'bout one more for the road?"

The bartender looks at him and then at me and Celeste. It's the first time he looks at us. He says, "Take your girls home, Frank." My father shimmers slightly, like a fast bolt of heat lightening has shot through him.

"What's the matter with you two?" My father has turned to look at us. "Don't you like your Shirley Temples? Do you want something else?"

We stare at our drinks. The fizz has gone out of them and the ice has mostly melted. There are black spots on my bright red cherries.

"I got you those, paid for them," he says. His finger taps on the bar. "Least you can do is drink up." His words are starting to melt together, not as bad as I know it will get, but it's the beginning.

Celeste starts to cry, just a little, a few tears sliding down her face and I still don't know what to do. He says, "OK, let's go." His voice is coarse. We follow him to the door and he opens it for us, saying, "After you, ladies." He is trying to be nice to us now, trying to lighten the mood. I know he is afraid I will tell my mother where we've been.

Just as we reach the car, it starts raining. It is sheets of rain, drenching us in a few seconds. Before we can even open the doors and get in the car, we are standing in puddles. My father swears softly under his breath. We get in and shut the car doors as he pulls out of the parking lot, as though he has forgotten we are with him. On the road, we can hardly see anything. Even the windshield wipers slamming back and forth as fast as they can aren't able to clear the rain. The scene from the car windows makes the world look like it is underwater and we are moving slowly, the way you do in water because of how strangely heavy it is.

It takes a long time to get home because the rain does not let up. "I have no visibility," my father keeps saying. "None at all." He is hunched over the steering wheel. I think he believes if he can get his face closer to the windshield, he'll be able to see better.

We have to park in the driveway when we finally get back because the garage door is down. This means my mother is home. My father swears again, softly, under his breath, but we can still hear him despite the rain pounding on the metal roof of the car, drum like. Celeste gets out and heads straight home. My father slides the two brown packages under the driver's seat. Later tonight he will come out to get them and he'll take them down to the basement, where he'll sit in an old rocking chair and drink.

Then he'll hide the bottles, one now half-empty, in the bottom drawer of a dresser in the cellar. He'll stumble up the stairs, fumble with the door, curse as he tries to open it.

I will try very hard to be asleep.

CHAPTER Five

Almost every morning at a certain hour, this blue jay tried to peck his way through my bedroom window. His orange claws, like scaly fingers, grasped the edge of the sill, and he pecked at the glass until his claws came loose, at which point he'd flutter around for a few seconds and then make another attempt to grasp and attack. He had been doing this for the past few weeks, beginning his assault while the sun was still at a slant, nowhere near fully risen. At first, Grace and I thought he was fascinating. Grace, always on a quest for tragedy, was certain the little thing was lonely, that his whole family had been sucked into a plane engine, and now he wanted to be a pet.

I took a dimmer view, seeing him as a deranged bird, maybe brain damaged from sailing head first into a sliding glass door, as blue jays do. I'll admit, whether traumatized or injured, there was a part of me that wanted to open the window and let him in, let him decide if we were the sort of household he was seeking. However, my mother made it clear that if we did that, she'd personally see to it that we spent every second of our free time cleaning up bird poo. It didn't seem worth it.

Now, after weeks of this behavior, Grace and I were both a little sick of it. Unless it was raining, we couldn't sleep past seven. I started building up a little resentment toward this bird, interesting as he was, and Grace complained that he was starting to give her nightmares.

The morning after the Great Beach Rescue, the bird was at it again. Grace turned over in bed and faced the wall, pulling the pillow over her head like a shield. I laid there for a while, trying to ignore the incessant rapping of the strong, sharp beak against the glass. I finally jumped out of bed and pressed my face against the window pane he was assaulting, scaring him witless. He fell off the sill, catapulting backwards and for a second I thought he was going to spiral to his death. He caught himself though, and flew off, disappearing into the foliage of the oak tree in the back yard, where I knew he would continue to watch the window, like a sentry, waiting for me to leave so he could return to his post.

Since I had no other options, I headed downstairs to the kitchen. My mother was pouring herself a cup of coffee, carrying on a conversation with Celeste.

"Morning," my mother said, "you're up early. Bird?"

"I'm ready to peg him with a BB gun," I told her.

"Claire," she said. "I don't like that language. And a blue jay, too, they're so cute."

My mother was the only person on the planet who actually thought blue jays were adorable, not the dregs of the bird world. I told her she was confusing jays with bluebirds.

"Bluebirds Mom, those are the nice birds. And a lot smaller. They probably wouldn't make so much noise."

"No BB guns, whatever kind of bird," she said, taking her coffee and heading out of the kitchen to get ready for work.

Celeste was sitting at the kitchen table, eating a bowl of cereal and reading the comics.

"Guess what we're doing this afternoon?" she asked me right off the bat, the way she always did, like we were perpetually in the middle of a conversation.

"What," I asked her. I dropped two slices of bread into the toaster and got a glass out of the cupboard and poured myself some orange juice from the carton on the table.

"We're going to Willie's house!"

"Good Lord. Why?"

"He wanted us to come over yesterday, but you were gone all day. So we're going over today, he's going to get off work early just for us, he's got something he wants us to see."

"Think about that statement Celeste," I instructed her. "Then ask yourself, 'is this really something I want to spend my time on?'"

Celeste had a remarkable ability to speak with just her face. Whenever I would disparage Willie Menard, she'd narrow her eyes, tighten her lips till they disappeared and raise one eyebrow. It was slightly harrowing, this look, but I was pretty staunch in my opinion of Willie. He was nice, but he was nineteen, just months away from no longer being a teenager, and he still lived with his father and showed no signs of ever moving on. Celeste was of the mind that he needed more slack than the average person because his mother had died in childbirth and he had been raised by a man who, though also nice, wasn't the brightest flame in the candelabra.

The two of them lived alone in the last house on the street, where the road ended and the woods began, a small copse that separated our street from the local high school. A wide creek flowed through their backyard, or at least it used to. They had spent so many years hauling junk from their house and dumping it all into the creek, the water was forced to make a new route for itself. They'd created some semblance of a pond in the backyard, a big pool of dead water that spawned half the mosquitoes born in our neighborhood.

Besides being a health hazard, the situation was pretty ironic, since Willie and his father ran a sort of hauling company. Anything you wanted to get rid of, they were your men! From roadside debris to ruined furniture, they'd load it up for you and take it to the dump. Their truck, which hadn't had a muffler on it for years, roared past our house every morning at five sharp. I asked Willie once what in the world there was to pick up at five o'clock in the morning.

"Road kill," he'd said, looking me dead in the eye as though there wasn't anything more critical than performing roughly the same job as buzzards. "Gotta clear 'em before morning traffic starts up. We got a police radio, one of those scanners, you know what those are? We listen for reports of deer and such and we go out and pick 'em up, haul the mess away. Send the bill to the county." He wouldn't tell me where the animals were dumped, like it was a big state secret. "You just leave it to us. You know what we like to say," and he repeated their company motto, which Willie had painted in big home-made letters on the side of their truck: You Maul It, We Haul It!

This was not a person I necessarily wanted to spend my precious time with, especially with summer coming to a fast close.

"What," I asked her. "What's he got?"

"I don't know, he said that's for him to know and us to find out."

"What do I do about Grace?" I asked her. "I'm supposed to watch her." I certainly wasn't going to bring Grace over there. I had my limits.

"Half an hour Claire, that's all. Half an hour. Put the TV on."

Celeste had a way about her, like she had a glowing coal in the middle of her chest instead of a heart. The heat was permeating, and it could make you feel sort of feverish, like you were coming down with the flu. I had never figured out how to counter her intensity. She liked Willie, or at least liked the idea of an older guy asking her to come over. There was something alluring about it, I guess. We'd gone over there before, many times, sitting in sagging lawn chairs by the rusty pond, maybe smoking a cigarette, drinking a beer. A classy pair, now that I think about it. No wonder Willie called us over once in a while. And I always gave in.

I told her all right, I'd go with her but we had to be back in time for Dark Shadows. Partly because I didn't want to miss it, but also so Grace wouldn't be sitting there watching Barnabas Collins all by herself, which would have been slightly worse than taking her over to Willie's house.

Grace came downstairs eventually and the three of us ate breakfast together, toast and juice and a couple of boiled eggs. My mother came in the kitchen after a while, ready for work. She put her coffee cup in the sink and before she left, she gave me a list of chores that had to be done before she got home, simple stuff that wouldn't keep me busy for long but I complained anyway since I knew she'd add to the list if she had any idea how easy she was making my life.

"I'm on vacation Mom, geez, give me a break. I won't have any time to do anything else. It's not fair, it really isn't." I made my voice shake and sucked in my bottom lip like I was about to burst out sobbing. As if. She seemed satisfied with my reaction, confident she was making me miserable.

"OK then, bye-bye," she said, a little too smug. Her blond hair swung around her shoulders as she bent to give each of us a kiss on the cheek, even Celeste.

Because we had nothing better to do, we started in on the list. And since all three of us got to work, it was still early morning when we finished and we had nothing left to do but sit around and wait until it was time for our date with Willie. The day dragged with the same momentum of a worm drying out on a hot sidewalk. The kind of boredom you enjoy because school is the only other option. By mid-afternoon, I set Grace up on the couch with a bag of chips and a soda. Celeste and I waited with her until some show was under way and we had promised her a thousand times we'd be home before Dark Shadows started.

"Cripes Claire," she said, "Just go already. I'm not a baby."

"I know," I said. And I did know. I had left her alone before, my parents didn't expect me to be right by her side every second of the day, but for some reason, it still made me nervous. I sometimes worried about the most pointless things.

Willie was waiting for us at the end of his driveway, watching as we walked down the street toward him, one hand behind his back, the other shoved all the way into one of the many pockets of his white carpenter pants. Willie was big, tall and broad shouldered, just the kind of person you'd picture pitching dead animals into the back of a truck, probably single-handed. He was wearing a used undershirt, the arm pits wet and worn.

"Nice of him to dress up for us," I mentioned to Celeste.

"Claire," she said to me, "God! Just be nice. It's not like I ask you for much."

"Glad you girls could make it," Willie said, eyeing us, but mostly Celeste.

Celeste and I looked a lot alike, except Celeste was slightly blonder, a little paler, a little smaller. I always joked that she was a ghost version of me. At fourteen, we weren't nearly as voluptuous as we thought we'd be by this age. I suppose whenever we looked at each other, we saw the same thing, a thin, pale girl, wondering where she'd be at the other end of her life. But we didn't mind not knowing, at least not yet. In each other, we saw possibility, the kind of possibility that is imprinted on you when you're born and takes years and years to fade.

We didn't approach things the same way, though. That was the big difference between us. My father told me once about a certain fish that lives in the left-over lava pools in Hawaii. No lie, they will fly right out of a pool and land smack in the middle of another pool, one they couldn't possibly have seen from the pool they were in.

"Think about that," my father had told me, "he not only has to know there's another pool of water in the spot he's going to land, but he has to figure it's better than the one he's in. Why do you think that is?" he asked.

"Um. It's some evolutionary flight response? The ticket to that species' survival?"

He looked at me like we'd never met. "Christ sake, Claire, I sometimes wonder where you get these ideas. Haven't I taught you anything? No. He's got faith," he said, looking at me hard. "He's got a lot of faith."

That was the kind of faith Celeste had. The kind that made her think maybe Willie had something to offer and that it was okay if he didn't, because there were plenty of other pools to fly into. And so today, she was fearless, excited from thoughts of breaking rules with Willie. She sauntered up to him and I held back a little, watching them. Willie smiled at her and then looked to me, still smiling but with slight worry in his eyes, afraid I wasn't as gung ho to join in. I shrugged my shoulders and stepped in line with Celeste, her fevered excitement like a contagion.

"What have you got behind your back, Willie?" Celeste asked, even before any of us could say hello, what's new.

Willie looked a little puzzled for a second, and then disappointed. Clearly he'd been planning on suavely introducing whatever it was he had behind his back, and now his plan had backfired thanks to Celeste. But he rallied.

"Well," he said, squaring his shoulders and running his free hand across his forehead, trying to get the hair out of his eyes. "Since you asked," and he pulled his other hand from behind his back. Squirming and clutching at his wrist was a kitten, tiny but shrill. We stared in silence for a moment, shocked at the image of Willie proudly trying to balance this little kitten in his hands, being careful not to let it drop. We'd expected a pack of cigarettes, maybe a couple cans of beer that he stole from his father. A kitten?

Celeste started squealing, her hands out like a beggar, taking the kitten from Willie's open hands, which were softly scratched from the kitten's needle-claws, thin lines of blood marking his hands and wrists like red thread, evidence of the trouble he'd had holding onto it while he waited for us. I have to admit, I got a little carried away, too, and it crossed my mind that it might have been all right to bring Grace along this time.

"Where'd you get him?" I asked, touching the kitten's head with one finger. There was no way this cat was the requisite eight weeks it was supposed to be. More like six, maybe even five, and I was wondering how Willie was able to feed it.

"At the dump," he said. "There was a whole litter of them. I couldn't find the mother anywhere, and I'll tell you, I searched for over half an hour." He had moved a step closer to us so he could touch it again. He put his hands on his knees, bending over slightly, so he was eye to eye with the tiny thing. "I think somebody must've just left them there. People do that, you know."

"Where are the others?" I asked him, a little worried, since I was pretty sure I already knew the answer.

"The pound," he said. Celeste sucked in her breath and I shook my head slightly at the thought. There was a moment of silence as we each contemplated the fate of the others. The animal shelter in our town wasn't much better than the dump. Maybe worse. Probably whoever had dropped the litter of kittens there had thought they were doing them a favor.

This wasn't the first time Willie and his father had found kittens at the dump. It was at least the fourth or fifth time they'd found a litter, sometimes it was kittens, more often it was a litter of puppies. Mr. Menard and Willie had sort of an agreement about the living trash they found when they hauled their truckloads of junk to the town dump. They'd ask around, maybe put a sign up at the grocery store and give away the ones they could. The rest were doomed. This was the first time they'd kept one for themselves.

"They'll be ok," he said. "That place is looking better, I swear. I really think they'll be all right." And for a moment I believed him. But his face was doubtful.

It occurred to me, for a brief moment, that this was perhaps why I didn't like Willie, why I joked about him, made fun of Celeste for wanting to hang out with him on summer afternoons when we didn't have anything better to do. It was the doubt I could see in his face. He had this honesty about him that he couldn't hide, like a really bad poker player. Most of us make life easy on ourselves. We have this cunning ability to make stuff up and eventually believe it, but not Willie. What do you call a person who can't lie to himself? Willie was the kind of person, when you looked at him, you saw how sorry a human being you actually were. That doubt that hung on his face, it was like a mirror, and you just had to see how heavily you doubted your own life.

Willie let Celeste carry the kitten to the backyard, where he had set up lawn chairs by the pond, red from the glare of the afternoon sun. The chair legs were spotted with rust, like they had been sprayed with rust-colored paint from an almost empty can. A pitcher of lemonade and three cups were set on a small table that had probably once been very nice. It was made of a heavy metal and painted white, but was now gouged and chipped and sat on the ground with a tilt. Sometimes Willie and his father kept some of the stuff that other people threw out, and some of it wasn't bad, like this table. We sat in the backyard for a while, the sun was warm without being overbearing, and the kitten entertained us with antics that kept us laughing until I looked at my watch and saw it was past time to go.

We hadn't left ourselves enough time. Most of the lemonade was still in the pitcher and Willie was just starting to tell us about this hoarder lady who got evicted and how much junk she had piled in her trailer, so much that she had dug trenches through the trash so she could walk around. I had to admit, I really wanted to hear the rest of it, but it was getting late and we had to go.

Willie was disappointed, "Why?" he asked, his voice too loud. I told him we never missed Dark Shadows, plus, I had to get back to Grace.

"That's true," he said. "You shouldn't leave her alone too long. A short time's ok, help her grow up a little, but you're right, not too long." And then the doubt was on his face again, grabbing me by the throat and telling me that Willie was not so bad, that it was ok to see kindness once in a while and to stop disapproving. "You disappoint me," his face said, but his voice was soft and gentle, hesitant, knowing that the truth can hit someone like a sledgehammer sometimes.

He picked up the kitten, whom we had decided he should name Burt, and held it against his face, holding one of its paws and waving it up and down in a tiny gesture of farewell. Willie said to come back soon, said it in a high pitched voice like the invitation was coming from Burt. Celeste laughed and looked at me.

I regret it. I regret leaving. I should have run home to get Grace. It would have been fine, it would have made her happy to play with Burt. I could have missed Dark Shadows for once. You could easily miss a week of it and get caught up in about five minutes. Celeste could have lived in her little dream world a few minutes longer. And Willie. Well. If I'd known this would be the last time we'd sit with him in his back yard, gazing over Lake Fetid, it would have been different. I would have raced home, told Grace that Willie had a great surprise for her, grabbed the bag of chips and gone back. We would have had a party.

That night at dinner, when my father asked what kind of day we'd all had, I didn't mention anything about the Menard's new cat. I knew Grace would only be disappointed that she didn't get to come with me, and my parents wouldn't want to listen to her whine about how she wanted to go see Burt. Grace filled them in on the theatrics that had gone on at Collinwood, that dark mansion on an island off the coast of Maine, where Victoria Winters was still trying to find out where she came from. It had actually been a pretty good episode. Once in a while they threw in a new twist, just to keep people watching.

"Hey, I've been thinking," my father announced. "That bird. I know why he's bugging you every morning."

Grace and I looked at him.

"It's the sun," he said. "When the sun starts coming up, it hits your window. It turns the window into a mirror and he sees himself. Blue jays, they're territorial, he's trying to dominate the other bird, only it's himself. He's fighting himself, his own reflection." He leaned back in the chair, arms crossed behind his head in a sort of self-satisfied pose, a little like Columbo after a big case. "Mystery solved," he said.

"Poor thing," my mother said. But Grace said he sounded pretty stupid. She was disappointed, I could tell. She preferred thinking he'd wanted to move in with us.

"He doesn't know any better," my father told her. My father told us that he'd stop soon, that he'd either give up, or get bored. He told us we'd never even notice when he was gone.

CHAPTER Six

Before we finished dinner that night, Mrs. Bergeron came over to return the pie plate. My mother invited her in, saying that her husband must be doing well, it seemed he at least had an appetite.

"I hope he liked the pie," my mother said, taking the empty pan from her hands. Grace and I sat up straight. It was like the candy man had just walked in. Grace immediately dropped her knife, making sure it slammed into her plate from a high enough height that it would bounce. We eyed Mrs. Bergeron, waiting for her to lose her noodle, but apparently it was going to take a bigger shock.

"Oh no," Mrs. Bergeron said, nodding in our direction and saying hello, "he can't eat a thing. He's still in pain. Just a lot of pills. He lost one whole finger, just a tiny nub of it left, and another half of one. I thank God it wasn't worse." She gazed up at the ceiling, as though God was just hanging there, and crossed herself, her imposing chest making it look like she had these little t-rex arms, which always cracked us up. "I've been trying to get some pea soup into him."

Of course. Pea soup. The perfect summer meal for people who have just been maimed. My mother asked her if she wanted to sit down and my father said he'd just made coffee. Mrs. Bergeron said thank you, she thought she had a few minutes to spare and sat down in the chair next to my father. She was wearing her blue tent dress that night, and I noticed it matched the color of our tablecloth. I had a brief vision of Mrs. Bergeron purchasing her clothing in the linens section of JC Penney.

"But the thing is, you know," she continued, "I don't exactly make the best pea soup." She turned to look at my father and gave him a deep sigh, as though that was the worst tragedy she could imagine.

"Well, I could make a pot," my father said, falling hard and fast into her trap. "I'll be cooking tomorrow anyway. I hear we're still doing the cookout, right?" As far as we knew, the plans for the cookout were going ahead, despite the fact that the power had come back on sometime Monday morning, soon enough to prevent anyone's meat from thawing out, even the people who kept opening their freezers every half hour. That's the funny thing about mass panic. When it gets into a mob's head that disaster is looming and they actually come up with a plan of action, it is so disappointing when the tragedy doesn't materialize.

It had been decided, for the sake of general neighborhood preparedness, to go ahead with the cookout. Partly because it would be fun, but partly to make sure that if we ever lost power for real, we'd know we could organize at a moment's notice.

"So, that's the other reason I came over," Mrs. Bergeron was saying. And here she straightened out her dress and touched her hair, as though she wanted to draw attention to something other than the request she was about to make. "Emile wants you to take the day off tomorrow." She sat down as my mother handed her a cup of coffee. She added enough cream to turn it almost white, and enough sugar to make it thick. A warm coffee milkshake.

"OK," my father said, "I was thinking of taking a vacation day, I was going to call him."

"Oh no, no," Mrs. Bergeron said, shaking her head like a dignitary. "He's going to comp you a day, he says not to worry about it, to just concentrate on organizing the neighborhood and, you know, your cooking."

It seemed expectations would be pretty high.

"Did you take one of your hams out of the freezer?" she continued. "Louis thought your ham salad would make a nice addition."

My father would freeze raw eggs before he'd freeze a ham, freezing sucked all the flavor out of it, but he said not to worry about a thing, if he had all day he could come up with something.

"Well, wonderful," Mrs. Bergeron continued. "The Gagnons thought maybe they'd bring their defrosted hamburger over in the morning and you could make your chili."

"I'd love to," he said.

Grace and I started clearing the dishes, leaving our parents and Mrs. Bergeron at the table with their coffee. Grace was as loud as humanly possible, but she didn't quite understand the way things worked. She didn't recognize the difference between a loud, obnoxious kid and the fright that comes from certain situations that appear all of a sudden.

"You're giving me a headache Grace," I told her, "cut it out."

"But I want to see Mrs. Bergeron throw something," she whispered back.

"That's not how it works," I told her. But it didn't matter, she continued to clatter plates and glasses together until the kitchen was clean and the adults were wrapping it up.

"Tell Emile thanks for the day off. I wanted to take the day anyway, I've got the Menards coming over to take that branch down, the one that's hanging right over the house. I'd like to be home when they're here."

"Didn't that get hit by lightning a while ago?" Mrs. Bergeron asked. My parents nodded and she said, "Well, you can't be too careful. Are they both doing it or are you getting up there Frank?" At this Mrs. Bergeron elbowed my father lightly in the ribs.

"He's afraid of heights," I said as I walked into the dining room, drying my hands on a dish towel to let them know the kitchen was clean. My mother added that he had vertigo, too, and wouldn't be climbing ladders any time soon and Mrs. Bergeron nudged him in the ribs again, like she couldn't get over how funny it was that my father couldn't climb a ladder. It was the one and only weakness he admitted to. "Well, isn't that how it is," she said, "the Good Lord didn't make any of us perfect, we all have a cross to bear, don't we?" After the adult ritual of saying good night fifty thousand times, Mrs. Bergeron thanked my father in advance for making the pea soup, and was finally out the door.

As soon as the door closed, my mother said she was grateful the neighborhood didn't want lobster stew for supper. "Look at it this way," my father said, looking right at me, "it gives me a chance to teach Claire how to cook." Before I could start complaining, he went down to the cellar to get his supplies and came up a few minutes later with his crock pot and a bag of charcoal. "Got some planning to do," he said, "you got any paper?"

I went upstairs and dug around in the back of the closet until I found a half used notebook from school. It was starting to get dark outside. For some reason, we slowed down in the summer, we never ate supper before seven and it seemed we sat around the table for hours. Night would sneak up on us without our noticing and all of a sudden it would be dark outside, the dim yellow street lamp having replaced the sun in silence. I wondered sometimes when, exactly, the day disappeared. But that evening, I did notice. I saw how the light had faded to a glow in my room, as though the sun, as it sank into the ground on the other side of the house, was grasping at tree limbs, the swing set, the house itself, anything that stood tall and solid, to save itself from slipping away.

I went downstairs and handed over the notebook along with a pencil stub.

"What are you going to make?" I asked.

"You mean we? Don't know yet. I was thinking of a ham salad, the chili of course, and maybe marinate the steaks tonight. And don't forget the pea soup. You'll help me, right?" he asked as he started to write out the menu.

I should have been proud. It wasn't everyone who would get a crack at my father's recipes, his techniques. I was the type to walk right past the Mona Lisa, he always said, and never take a second look. But I said, ok, I'd help. I didn't really have anything else to do.

So he pulled out two cutting boards and we started chopping. It was a haphazard process as far as I could tell, but then I wasn't the expert. We made piles of garlic and onion, green and red peppers, all separated from each other because they cooked at different speeds. We poured steak sauce and balsamic vinegar into a Tupperware container, added olive oil, minced garlic, rock salt and peppercorns that we smashed with a hammer, splitting them open and letting them settle to the bottom of the bowl, and we placed a cut of sirloin on top, shaking the plastic tub to get the steak completely covered. He bought these ingredients, his staples, at Poverelli's, a small Italian grocery store in Portland that we discovered one day purely by accident while we were shopping for my mother's birthday. We ended up buying her a string of garlic and red peppercorns that year. Unearthing that shop was one of the best things that ever happened to my father, as far as I knew.

"Don't know what I would have done if I hadn't stumbled on that store," he was saying, the same thing he said whenever he was busy in the kitchen, chopping, pouring, mixing his ingredients like an alchemist, turning mediocre cuts of steak, gray chicken legs bought on their sell-by dates, even vegetables, into meals that made colors more vibrant. It made worn out stories more interesting. His food could make stupid jokes funny.

He poured boiling water over dried red kidney beans and set them at the far end of the counter. He'd put the soaked beans in the crock pot early in the morning and would add the Gagnon's hamburger once the beans started getting soft, along with the peppers, onions, garlic and a piece of burnt orange peel that he'd put in the oven that night, browning it till the edges curled. "There has to be a mystery in every dish," he'd say, "something that gets people wondering what that flavor is." A few hours before it was ready, he'd add tomatoes that he'd roast in the oven first and he'd say it again, ingredients cook at different rates of speed, you can't add everything all at once. "Mark of an amateur," he'd tell me. "Oh. And Claire, don't forget to fish that orange peel out of the chili before we serve it. We don't want to give away our secrets."

It was late by the time I finally got to bed, but at least we had gotten most of the prep work done. In the morning we'd have to get a ham, but we had minced the pickles, pimentos and onions that would go into the salad, mixing them together and putting them in the refrigerator so the flavors could meld. He'd put the ham bone in a pot with onions and salt and let that simmer for about three hours before he added the split peas. There was no mystery to pea soup because sometimes simplicity is complicated enough.

My hands smelled like a mix of fresh vegetables and vinegar that I couldn't wash off, even seeping through the heavy almond scent of Jergens lotion. They say that smell is the sense most closely associated with memory. That night in our kitchen, preparing our disproportionate part of the neighborhood meal, was a vision that would rise up whenever I smelled pickles or onions, or any other mixture of smells we created that night. The scene in our kitchen, my father's soft voice as he told me what to do, would never stray far from my mind. So easy to remember, like cutting an onion.

CHAPTER Seven

B y the time I got up the next morning, Willie was already there. I woke to the sound of a ladder slamming into the side of the house and for a moment, I thought the branch had broken off at last. Then I heard my father say good morning, the screen door slamming shut so I figured he had gone outside to supervise the Menards. It occurred to me that I didn't know where exactly they were putting the ladder, so just in case they were going to shimmy it near my window, I decided to get up. I got dressed quickly, or as quickly as I could with my heart racing, fingers fumbling from the panic that Willie's face would suddenly appear in my window.

I made my way down the stairs and found Grace in the kitchen. My father was still outside and my mother was at work.

"Dad and I went shopping already," Grace informed me, "while you were asleep." She gave me a snotty look, implying that they hadn't needed me to help pick out the ham.

"Good," I said. "I hope you got a good one, not too salty." Her hair was done in a French braid, she must have gotten up before my mother left for work.

"The bird woke you up again, didn't it?" I asked her.

"How do you know? You were sound asleep when I got up. You don't know everything." Grace looked at me with an earnest stare, like she was trying to make a point. "You don't know everything, Claire," she said again.

"Yes I do. Your hair's done, which means you got up before Mom left because you can't do it by yourself, and the only thing that wakes you up that early is the bird. See? I'm Sherlock Holmes."

There was a strangeness to that day. I can remember each instance with the same clarity you see in the split second of a lightning strike. I can recall, as plainly as though I were still standing there in the kitchen, the look on my sister's face when I said that to her, a look of resignation, almost futility. As though, all at once, she had decided not to argue with me anymore. I don't know if it was the first time such a look registered on her face, or only the first time I noticed it.

My father came in and Willie walked in behind him. The screen door slammed again, the sound made him cringe and he said sorry.

"Never mind," my father said, "it does that."

"I could fix that for you," Willie said. "Maybe after we take care of that branch." Willie turned back toward the door, opening and closing it as he pulled on the sagging spring that hung like an old clothes line from the top. "I could just replace all this hardware, give you a little more tension when you close the door, and then it won't slam so hard."

Like everything in our house, the screen door was old. A lot of things needed fixing or replacing and each one represented a project my father was 'just getting to.'

"I was thinking of maybe getting a new door," my father told him.

"Yeah, I can see that," Willie told him, "sometimes it's out with the old, in with the new, as they say." Willie's hair was cut unevenly, long over one ear but shorter over the other. It hung down over his eyes but was shorter in the back. He made me think of what a scarecrow might look like if it was made by a bunch of little kids without adults interfering. Even his clothing looked draped across his frame, nothing he wore ever fit him exactly right.

"So. When will your father be here?"

"Oh, he's coming along in a minute," Willie said. "He told me to go ahead and get set up."

They started talking about how Willie and his dad were going to manage the tree and I turned my attention away, since all this man-talk was getting on my nerves. When I looked at Grace, who was still staring at me with her pointed expression, I remembered Burt. "Hey, I know what will cheer you up, Grace," I told her. "Hold on." I interrupted my father, who had moved onto a discussion of the tools that would be used to cut the branch, to ask Willie if he'd brought the cat.

"Jeez, I just about forgot her," he said. "I got her in the truck outside. Go and get her if you want, I thought Grace might want to play with her, seeming's how Burt was such a great hit yesterday." He winked at my father, the way a grown man might. And that's another moment I remember so clearly, like Willie was still standing right in front of me, wearing the same work pants he'd worn the day before, moving his hair out of his eyes the way he always did. Winking at my father, a shrewd smile on his face, as though he were secretly communicating something important. Because today he was a man. He had a truck, a ladder and a job, and that made him kin to men. No longer my equal, but my father's.

I told Grace to come with me and we rushed outside. Leave it to Willie to forget about a kitten in a hot truck. But he had parked in the shade and left the windows open a little, so it was fine. It wasn't too hot out and there was a breeze that sailed through the air and moved the arms of the weeping willow in our yard so it appeared to be dancing. I got Burt out of the truck and carried her to the willow tree, where I set her down under the sway of the thin branches that dropped low to the ground, low enough so the kitten could reach them. Grace forgot she was mad at me and sat on the grass by my side, holding a broken branch from the willow tree and shaking it over the kitten's head, making her jump. She had that cat twirling like a wind-up toy, shrieking with laughter whenever Burt lost her balance and fell over. I didn't even have to do anything entertaining, the two of them were so enchanted with each other.

Willie and my father came outside after a few minutes, stopping on the porch steps briefly while my father pointed out the sagging boards. Willie stood in the middle of one step and bounced up and down, like he was on a diving board. "I could fix that, too," I heard him say and my father nodded his head and said they'd talk about it.

From where I sat in the front yard, I could see the backs of them as stood side by side and looked up toward the roof.

"That ladder looks a little close to the house," I heard my father tell him. "I think it needs to be set farther out, at more of an angle." My father spoke with his hands and I knew he was trying to stress that the foot of the ladder was too close to the house.

Willie grabbed it with both hands and gave it a shake. "It's a good sturdy ladder," he said, giving it another violent shake, completely ignoring the point. They had a short, manly conversation about ladder placement and my father managed to convince Willie to move the ladder to the side of the house so he wouldn't be crawling up the steep slant of the roof.

"Bit higher to climb, but that will put you closer to the tree branch. And you won't be dragging your gear so far."

"No problem," Willie said, giving the ladder another violent shake. "This ladder goes all the way up to eighty foot, she's adjustable. Ever seen one of these? They go anywhere." My father told him to give a shout when his dad showed up. "You need a cup of coffee Willie?" my father asked him. "No," he shook his head slightly, "I'm good."

That day. It should have continued vying to become the most boring day of my life. It should have been a day like so many others, a series of lost events that I'd never remember. If Willie hadn't seen me watching him, maybe he would have waited for his father, I don't know. I couldn't tell if he was embarrassed about not being allowed to work on his own, but he fiddled needlessly around the truck for a while. He got out the chainsaw, a heavy, mean-looking machine with a notched chain that wouldn't have a problem gnawing through the branch. He could have taken the whole tree down with that thing. He shook the ladder a few more times and then decided that he'd go ahead and move it himself.

He stood between the ladder and the house, hoisting it with one arm and balancing himself against the side of the house with the other. But the ladder was long and awkward, and he walked unsteadily, like a drunk. At one point he stumbled backward as the top of the ladder started to swing downward and he lost some of the progress he had just made. He started moving forward after he got the ladder balanced again. I asked him if he needed any help and I started to get up from the ground.

"I got it Claire. It's not heavy, just a little hard to balance. Bitch of a ladder, pardon my French. Thanks though."

My father didn't come back outside and Mr. Menard never showed up and I suppose Willie thought he needed to get started. His only other choices were to stand around looking stupid or sit with me and Grace on the lawn which, even I have to admit, would have been a little childish. And so he started up the ladder.

In my mind, I see it over and over again, what happened next. But sometimes, my mind takes a different tack, and I can change what happened. Now, sometimes, when I think back on it, I tell Willie to wait for his father. His father finally shows up and checks the ladder, sets it correctly, holds it for Willie as he climbs. Now, when I fix everything, Willie's father can be the one who carries the mean-looking chainsaw up to the roof and hands it easily to Willie, who takes it from him and then helps his father climb to the safety of the roof. In my mind, when I think back on it, I fix everything. But that day, what really happened was that Willie shook the ladder one final time and trusted that a strong set of rungs is all a person needs to safely climb to the top of a house.

He took the chainsaw up with him, and I really did almost tell him to leave the chainsaw, to just take the coil of rope he had around his shoulders. I even got part way up from where I was sitting on the lawn, but I didn't. I was afraid he'd think I was flirting with him and the thought embarrassed me. And so Willie climbed. He made it almost to the top, his head was just reaching the roof line when he hesitated. It is at this point that he must have realized he'd forgotten to adjust the ladder. The ladder was lined up a little lower than the peak of the roof, but he hadn't adjusted it. It was still fixed for the lower height he had originally set it.

He was caught in a moment, one of those moments when you realize you have not thought something all the way through. Just moving from the ladder to the roof was hard enough, but to do it with a chainsaw was even harder. He stepped up one more rung, the top rung, one hand on the roof, and swung the chainsaw a little behind him to get the momentum he needed to lift it up to the roof, and that small motion moved the ladder. It rocked slightly backward, away from the house, and then sideways as Willie tried to throw the chainsaw onto the roof and then backwards again as the big machine fell from his grip. He made a grab for the edge of the roof as the ladder fell over, having finally made up its mind about which way to fall. It fell sideways, toward us, and clattered to the driveway with the peeling sound of a bell. Willie held onto the edge of the roof and at first it looked like he was going to be able to pull himself up.

Grace and I screamed together. One of us screamed for Willie to hold on, the other screamed for my father and I couldn't tell which voice was hers and which was mine. My father flew out the door, faster than possible, hurtling off the porch without touching the steps, coffee sloshing out of his cup as he screamed back at us, saying what's wrong, what happened? Who got hurt?

Willie fell. It took my father a few seconds to register what that sound was, first the loud, sudden cry and then the heavy dull sound right behind him. He turned and saw Willie lying on the driveway, on his side, his face turned away from us.

He put his hands over our faces. "Get in the house! Get in the house!" he screamed at us. It was hard to move, but he grabbed me by the shoulders and told me to take Grace inside and call for an ambulance.

We stumbled up the porch steps. At first I couldn't open the screen door, I kept pushing it when I needed to pull it open. Grace had to get me out of the way and pull the door open so we could get inside. My hands were shaking so hard, I could hardly grip the phone and I stared at the dial, forgetting everything I'd learned about calling for help. Grace told me to dial zero and when the operator came on the line, she told me to say we needed an ambulance. And then my little sister, the one who couldn't even brush her own hair, told me to call Mom and then she said that maybe we needed to call Mr. Menard, too.

CHAPTER Eight

Willie had died, there was no question. But when the EMT, a young man with a mustache so thin it should have embarrassed him, shook his head and told the people standing in the driveway, "No, I'm sorry," no one believed him. At least not at first. Maybe he just looked too young and inexperienced. Or maybe, because of his childish mustache, they thought, briefly, he was fooling around and they were waiting for him to say, "Just kidding!" But then Mr. Menard hit the pavement, knees first, and then all the way down, his head resting on the driveway only a few feet from where Willie lay.

Mr. Gerard and Mr. Bergeron were the only men there when the ambulance showed up, besides my father. Everyone else was at work. So it was the women who took over. When Mr. Menard folded and then began to wail, Mrs. Bergeron knelt on the ground and put her arms around his shoulders, hugging him a little. The others, all mothers of the little kids in the neighborhood, stood in line behind her, like they were at the grocery store, patiently waiting their turn.

The men paced, white faces and agitated hands, saying over and over how could this have happened, how could this be? How could a ladder just fall over, as though there were no such thing as gravity. My father worried me. He walked around the ambulance, around and around, like the hand of a clock, the same circular route that didn't vary, because time is going to move forward no matter what, and you might as well move along with it. You don't have a choice. Even when my mother arrived, frantic because I think I just told her there was an accident, nothing else, he didn't stop walking in the circle he had made.

Grace and I stood side by side in the window, watching them all. Their bewilderment and their grief etched in each face, too sharp to be real, like the facets in a diamond.

"What do we do?" Grace asked me.

"I don't know. Just wait, I guess."

We waited while the paramedics loaded Willie's body onto a stretcher and into the back of the ambulance. I was surprised to see that they really did use black bags, just like on TV. We waited while the women got Mr. Menard on his feet and walked him back to his house. And waited as my father talked to the police officers who had shown up, watching as one of them took notes in a little notebook that he tucked back into his shirt pocket when he was done.

I had to talk to the police because I was the only one who witnessed the accident. I only told them what I saw. I told them everything Willie did; he moved the ladder, he stumbled, he climbed, he dropped the chainsaw and it broke into pieces on the driveway. He fell. I didn't mention that I almost got up to tell Willie to wait for his dad. I didn't tell them I, too, had failed to notice that he hadn't set the ladder to a safe height. I didn't mention that the only thing I did manage to do was scream when it was all just too late.

When our house and yard were finally empty of the authorities, the neighbors began to arrive. They rang the doorbell, making it chime endlessly in the house until my father ripped the mechanism off the wall. Two wires, one red, one white, stuck out of the hole, tiny copper threads, mangled, exposed at the ends. One more thing we could have had Willie fix. My father didn't have the men come inside, he went out and stood on the porch with them. Mr. Gerard held the meeting, which lasted about fifteen minutes and involved a lot of smoking, head nodding, and abrupt violent embraces.

It was bright day, but it looked dark out to me. The cigarette ends glowed brighter than they should in the daytime. Everything was so quiet. Even though I was in the living room and the window was open, I could only hear the men whispering quietly when they were outside on the porch, like fish gurgling under water. And when my father came in and started talking to us, I had to strain to hear him, even though he was right in front of me. We were going to go ahead with the neighborhood cookout, he told us. Only now we were calling it a wake. It made sense to me, holding a wake. In times of trouble, the neighbors brought food to whomever needed it anyway. Plus, the neighborhood would have been buzzing about what had happened and would have been burning up the phones lines with their questions as the families tried to piece the story together. Killing two birds with one stone would make the night run a lot smoother.

But it was sad. The kitchen was heavy. It was heavy with the smell of cooking, heavy with the sound of the meat grinder rasping out strings of meat that fell into a bowl where it sat until I mixed in mayonnaise and the onion mixture my father and I had made the night before. "Are you doing okay?" my father asked me. I told him I was. But after I finished with the ham salad, I went upstairs to lay down on my bed and no one bothered me. I lay on my side the way Willie had lain on his side after he fell, and stared out the window. I thought back to that morning, when I almost fell over in my rush to get dressed, certain I would see Willie's face appear as he climbed the ladder. Wishing, at that moment, that it would appear now and feeling somehow guilty that the window stayed empty, the view to the tops of the trees in the yard unblocked. I would have prayed to God to start the day over, to give me a chance to fix everything, but I didn't because I knew it wouldn't help, that I'd just be embarrassing myself. Not even God can go up against time.

I lay there until I heard the house start to come alive. The door opened and slammed shut, and I was reminded that Willie was going to fix the door for us. I wondered if every time it slammed shut, I would think of this day. I heard pounding up the stairs and Celeste came in. Right away, I could tell it was killing her that she hadn't been outside with us when it happened. She had that panicked, breathless air about her. "I can't believe it," she cried, sinking on my bed. "It's my mother's fault. She made me clean my room and I will never forgive her for that, swear to God. So tell me, what happened?"

It's a weird trick of human nature, this knack for turning the witnesses of tragedy into automatic celebrities. I thought she was about to ask for my autograph, the way she started gushing about how scared I must have been, did the ladder almost hit me? How close had I come to death? And it is a sad piece of human nature that makes us latch onto anything that might give us that star status. I felt like

Queen Mary. I told her all about it. I told her the beginning, about how Willie was acting like a pseudo-man in front of my father, like he was so much bigger than me, how he said he was going to fix everything in the house. I told her the middle, how Willie staggered under the weight of the ladder and set the ladder against the house all wrong. And I told her the end, about how he dropped the chainsaw, how the ladder fell from under him, and how he landed, dull and heavy.

"I heard all the noise," she said, "but my mom wouldn't let me come over. She said it sounded bad, the way you were screaming and everything." It felt right somehow, that I would have been the only witness, the last to see him alive, the last to be seen by him. It felt like Willie belonged to me.

It took Grace to put everything back into perspective. She came into our room with Burt, the kitten sound asleep against her chest, and that made everything feel dark and quiet again.

"That's Willie's cat," Celeste whispered. "What are you going to do with her? You can't keep her, you should let me take it." Celeste knew our family rule, or what I told her was our family rule, that we weren't allowed to have animals in the house. I told Grace it was because our mother was allergic.

Grace started to cry, huge wrenching sobs rising out of her. I want to keep her, she kept saying over and over. Just let me keep her. But Celeste told her, carefully told her, that she couldn't have her, that Willie had said if anything ever happened to him, that he wanted her, Celeste, to take care of Burt. "But he said you're her godmother, and to make sure to let you come over and play with her whenever you want." And that she was supposed to bring the cat over every day, if possible, to let Grace play with it. "That's what he told me, Grace. And I swear, I'll let you play with her every day, she'll just sleep at my house. But you keep her for now, you keep her until it's time for me to go home." And such was the kindness of Celeste.

We waited for Grace to stop crying before we went downstairs to help set up the charcoal grills and folding tables and chairs. Since we lived right next door to the Bergeron's, the neighbors had started setting up grills and tables between our two houses. The charcoal had already been lit since it took a while for the flames to die down and the coals to get red hot and the air smelled acrid, the way it does on hot summer days before the meat starts cooking. Mr. Gerard and Celeste's father were carrying a cooler, each of them holding a handle. It looked heavy, the way it banged their legs as they carried it, and when they set it down, it dropped like an anchor. I figured it must have been loaded down with ice and beer, maybe a few sodas for the kids.

The sun was still out, since it was August, and it would stay light out till much later. But long shadows were starting to cross the street, the sun making the shadows of the houses and trees appear lanky, like dark reflections in a funhouse mirror. Lawn chairs were set up in clusters and some people had already lit their Coleman lanterns in anticipation of the darkness. It smelled like lighter fluid and bug spray mixed with Avon bath oil. Mr. Menard's house remained still and dark, it looked empty. I wasn't sure whether anyone had informed him that we were now holding a wake for Willie, so it made me nervous that he might think we were going ahead with festivities as planned. But he came outside eventually. He walked down his driveway and turned toward us at a slow gait and we watched him, silent, as he approached. He looked stooped and small. He wasn't a very big man, nowhere near as big as Willie, and now he looked even smaller. Celeste's mother got him a beer from the cooler, her heels clinking on the road as she hurried toward him. Everyone got up and walked to him, shaking his hand, hugging him, like he was a war hero just returned home.

Everyone felt like they had to give him something, a handshake, a beer, a plate of pimento cheese and crackers, as though they were all responsible, somehow, for having taken Willie away. Only my father stayed where he was. He stayed standing in front of the charcoal grill, staring at the flames that reached higher than the grate. He watched the flames for as long as it took them to die down to small flames that curled around the coals, exhausted from their wild dance. He was still watching until they disappeared completely, until all the beauty of the flames had vanished and only the grey ash of the hot coals remained. He watched the flames and I watched him.

Here was my fear, a fear that grew like fire. The fear that this was an event my father couldn't get past, that Willie's death would set him ablaze and he would drink to put the fire out. So I watched.

Celeste dragged two lawn chairs over to where I was sitting. Grace was behind her, struggling with one chair as she still held the sleeping Burt in one hand.

"Here Claire," said Celeste, "take one of these chairs. Why are you sitting on the grass?" I unfolded one chair and picked up the one Grace had dropped.

"Can you do this chair for me Claire," she asked me, "I don't want to drop the cat."

The three of us, finally settled in the lawn chairs at the foot of my driveway, took in the scene. Mr. Menard was holding a plate of food in each hand and an unopened can of beer under his arm. It looked as though someone had played a practical joke on him, telling him to hold these plates, and this beer, and then leaving him to wander around, searching for a place to set everything down so he could actually eat. It would have been funny, like a sit-com episode, something the three of us would have gotten a big kick out of. But now, given the circumstances, it was just sad. I wanted to get up and take the plates from him, hold them in my own hands until someone got a folding table set up. But I couldn't go near him. I wouldn't have known what to say. I wouldn't even have been able to speak. So I told Celeste to get up and help him. Mrs. Bergeron and my mother were putting a checkered table cloth over two poker tables they'd pushed together, and Celeste took the two plates of food from him. They put a chair at the table for him, and my mom took him by the arm to lead him to his seat.

He dropped the can of beer he was still holding under his arm and when it hit the ground, beer started to fizz out. That's another thing we would have found hilarious. We would have sat there watching Mr. Menard pick it up, praying it would explode in his hands, and this would have given us the great idea of shaking all the cans of soda and beer in the cooler, setting us up for high entertainment the rest of the night. But on this night, when the can hit the ground and started hissing, Burt jumped off Grace's lap to investigate the noise. And when

Mr. Menard saw the cat, his face seemed to crack and start leaking. He cried silently, on his knees, tears mixing with spit that pooled on the street where he kneeled, the kitten cradled in his hands. He pressed her against his chest the way a sinner holds the rosary. When he could speak, he said, "My boy. This is my boy's cat." Over and over.

That was the point where we realized, all of us, all at once, that we had lost Willie. Loss is such a strange thing. It is a great magnifier, it makes whatever we've lost appear larger than it ever would have been. To be honest, if Willie was there that night, we would hardly have noticed him. He would have eaten a huge plate of food, complimented my father on the steak and winked at us whenever some little kid opened a can of Fresca and it detonated all over his face. He would have gone home early because he had to get up at five in the morning and all the mothers would have shaken their heads after he'd gone and wondered out loud how in the world he was ever going to meet some girl and get married. And that would have been it. Taking someone for granted, it's a secret gift.

My father didn't seem to notice any of this. He put the steak on the grill and stared at it for a few minutes. He walked to the picnic table that he and my mother must have dragged to the front yard, and stirred the chili. A long orange extension cord stretched from the garage and his crock pot along with someone else's was plugged into it. When he stirred the pot, I could smell it and that reminded me I hadn't fished out the orange peel. I wanted to just sit on my chair, to not move, but there had to be some distraction from Mr. Menard, so I got up and stood next to my father.

"That chili came out pretty good Dad, I can tell by how it smells."

"Yes," he said, "I think it's not bad."

"I forgot to fish out the orange peel, by the way."

"Shoot, Claire! What if someone finds it? What then, huh?" And he started digging around for it with a wooden spoon and I felt better, now that he had something to do.

The rest of the night was quiet. All the adults took turns comforting Mr. Menard, who eventually stopped crying and picked at his plates of food. My father was the last to approach him. He brought the steak over, setting the platter on the table right in front of him.

"I made a steak," he said, stating the obvious. I guess he didn't know what else to say, but it seemed to be the right thing. Mr. Menard nodded his head and said, "Willie always liked your steak."

"I know he did," my father said. "I don't think I ever told you, but once, when Willie was little, he smelled my steak cooking on the grill. We were having a cookout, it was a family reunion and he came over. Asked if he could stay for supper."

"Did he now?" Mr. Menard smiled at that and shook his head. "He was such a cute little kid. No fear, that one. No manners either, but I never minded."

"I told him, sure anytime. I told him he was welcome anytime. He was one of the family."

"Nice of you," Mr. Menard said. "He fit right in, didn't he? Doesn't surprise me. Everyone loved him. Everyone." His voice was low but it carried across the yard. Everyone was quiet, letting Mr. Menard have the floor. Let the grief stricken talk, get it all out. That was the kind of medicine we practiced.

"He was a good boy," my father told him, "we all thought he was a good boy."

And the neighbors nodded and murmured their assent. It was as though someone had unblocked a storm drain. Mr. Menard started talking about Willie, telling us more about him than we ever knew, more than we ever could have known. And by the end of that night, we cared more about Willie than we probably ever would have. That's another thing I would learn about loss, it starts as a great emptiness, a deep well. We fill it first with grief and when that drains, we fill it with anger. When that has seeped into the ground, it stays filled with memories. For a while. Everything will eventually be forgotten, just ask my uncle. But it leaches into the ground gradually, so you don't notice it, until all that's left is soft spot in the ground.

It is cold.

Very cold. It is a dark night, no moon, but somehow there is a glow in the room and I can see the shapes of things. I have already doubled my down comforter and yet I still shiver, so I get out of bed, the comforter around me like a shawl, and crawl into bed with Grace. With two blankets, it will be warm enough. But she isn't there. Her bed is empty and it takes me only a second to know where she is.

With my quilt still around me, I go downstairs. I kneel in front of the hall closet, and with my hands, I find my boots and put them on. Outside, the air is so cold it freezes my lungs and it's hard to breathe. In my frozen voice, I call her. I sound like ice. Her voice, too, is thin and brittle. She does not answer me, but calls out for her dog, her new dog, the one Willie gave her. The one he found at the dump, along with its litter mates, shaking in the cold, wagging their tails and licking his hands, their savior. He has given us one of the puppies, a small brown dog, long hair that hides its face, obscures all its features. Grace has chosen a name both complicated and typical. Mr.Snuffleupagus. We call him Snuffy, and this is the name she calls out now, in the middle of the night, in the freezing air.

The cold is seething. I find my sister and try to bring her inside. She also wears a shawl made of her down comforter, but she is in her slippers, princess slippers, and the snow is making her feet blue.

I can't find him. I can't find him. She repeats these words over and over in a voice wrought with fear.

You can't stay out here, I tell her. You'll freeze. She is only three, so she does not realize this. She doesn't understand.

But it is too bitter outside, a biting cold that would kill us if we let it. I take her in the house and she can hardly walk, her feet are so stiff.

It will be all right, I tell her, dogs know to find safe places. I don't know why Daddy did that, she says. I just don't know why. She is too little to understand the nonsensical act of a drunk when he is angry. She is too young to recognize the creeping rage of a drunk, the kind of rage that can't be cooped up for a hundred years like a genie in a bottle, a malignant force that looks for any reason to break free. She is too small and lovely to realize that you don't play with your new puppy in the living room until he is crazy with happiness so that he can't control himself and he barks and wets the carpet.

My father takes the puppy by the back of the neck and throws him out. Throws him off the porch and into the snow, where the little dog, despite his size, breaks through the crust that has formed on the powder and disappears for an instant before he bounds up, still crazy with happiness. For a while he is probably happy in the snow, until he realizes the porch light is out and he is alone. We can hear him whine at the door, we can even hear him scratching, but no one dares to go outside and get him. Even Grace waits until it is dark and quiet in the house.

I put her in bed and tell her I will take a turn, that I will look for him. And I do. I go outside and call for him and listen hard for any sound. I tell myself, as I told Grace, that he will find a place to stay warm and I get myself to believe it enough that I can go back in before I freeze to death.

My father is the one who finds him. He finds him the next morning when he opens the door to take the bottle of bourbon from the taxi driver he has called, his own personal delivery man. My good man, he says, my thanks. Please, take my thanks. The taxi driver says he will also take his money, if he doesn't mind. The puppy is right there, on the porch. We can't see him from inside the house but my father says What's this? He loses his balance and falls over, catching himself with his hands so he only falls to his knees. Grace and I crowd the doorframe, my mother looking over the top of our heads. She gasps, a guttural sound, and pulls us back into the house, but not before we see that my father has found him.

Grace's little dog is curled up and looks like he's sleeping. Hey! What do ya know, it's Snuffy! My mother jerks us back into the house before we can see my father reach out and touch him, to try and wake him up. But we see my father recoil. And then recover. He laughs, a wheezing kind of chuckle, as though his lungs are freezing in the cold morning air. Snuffy! He laughs so he can hardly speak. Snuffy...Snuffy...Snuffy snuffed it! Get it? Snuffed it? He laughs, still on his knees but struggling to get up. The taxi driver backs down the steps. He is horrified and hurries back to his warm taxi, which he has left running in the driveway.

CHAPTER Nine

The picnic table was still in the front yard, but it was the only thing that was out of place. The grills had all been put away, as well as the folding tables and chairs. And the ladder. I hadn't noticed when that had been moved off the driveway and I didn't know who had taken it. Mr. Menard probably would not have wanted it back, so it would most likely become the neighborhood ladder. Whenever any family needed it, they'd get it from whoever had used it last and every time it was taken out and set up, they'd be reminded of Willie. He would be everywhere, in every home project, in every shutter that got repainted, in every garage light that lit up the darkness when someone came home late.

I sat at the picnic table. The wood was splintered and the redwood stain was faded and worn away from all the time the table had spent outdoors. But it was only eight years old, I remembered when we got it, the summer Grace was born. My father had borrowed the Menard's truck to pick it up from the hardware store. Even back then, Willie had been overly helpful, offering to stain the table for us, I remembered him getting really excited about it, like staining picnic tables was the height of summer entertainment and he looked so disappointed when his father told him to settle down. I wondered, as I sat there, whether everything I ever looked at for the rest of my life would have a piece of Willie in it.

The street was quiet, my father had already left for the morning shift and it was too early for anyone else to be heading to work. It was cool outside, like it was every morning, with a clear sky. It was the type of morning where you could sit outside and just think because there was nothing around to bother you. Maybe a few chickadees calling back and forth to each other, morning being their favorite time of day. They chattered from inside the green foliage of the trees, invisible, like tiny little ghost birds.

They didn't bother me. I was thinking about my father. There's a kind of worry that eats at you if you have a father who drinks. It's like boot camp for bomb diffusers. One wrong move, cut the wrong wire, get lazy for a split second and it's all over. An explosion will rip you apart. All you can do is throw yourself onto the device and hope it doesn't tear up everything around you. Willie's fall from the roof of our house, it was a trigger, the mechanism that could set off an explosion. I saw Willie fall, over and over. And I knew my father heard his children screaming, saw our faces, felt the vibration under his feet when Willie landed. Over and over. He would think it was his fault, as sure as if he had pulled the ladder away himself. He'd think it was all his fault. Because he had vertigo. He couldn't climb a ladder and take down his own tree limb.

So here was my plan. I would keep watch, pay attention to my father's movements, notice if he came home late, where he went in the house, where he'd poke around outside. I'd look for his bottles of whiskey, find them, and pour them out. Cut the wires.

And then there were his pills. My parents had no idea I knew what antabuse tablets were, but I did. They were pills he was supposed to take every morning, pills that would make him throw up if he had a drink, like ipecac for adults. A few times, I'd caught my mother checking the pill bottle, making sure the bottle was not staying full. I did the same thing. But now I would check every single day and make sure he was taking them, check the trash can in the bathroom, make sure they weren't in there. If I found any, I would take them out and grind them up, put them in his thermos of coffee he took to work every day. Cut the wires. You just had to make sure you cut the right ones.

And then it occurred to me that the house was quiet now, with my father gone to work and Grace and my mom still asleep. I could start now, make a cursory sweep of the house and the cellar, check the pill bottle. I started with the garage, since I was already outside.

Along the back wall of the garage was a workbench, or something that was originally intended to be a workbench. You'd have to dig under a pile of rubble to find a hammer. In the summer, it was one of my father's hiding places. There were makeshift plywood doors under the bench, latched shut with small sliding bolts. I opened each door and sucked in my breath at the sound the rusty hinges made, squealing in that particular pitch that feels like an ice pick in your head. Everything on the shelves had a coating of rust, nothing that looked new. It was a mixed smell of turpentine and spilled paint. It was a jumble of old paintbrushes and rags that hadn't been cleaned well enough and so were stiff with paint, unusable. Old paint cans sealed with rust were draped in cobwebs. A daddy longlegs strode across the top shelf, his legs thin as hair. Nothing was hidden inside and so I closed the doors, sliding the latches shut so there'd be no sign I was there.

In the house, I checked the bathroom first. The bottle of pills was in the cabinet and there weren't any in the trash, both good signs and I felt like I'd been given an all-clear signal. But you could never be too sure. I could have overlooked something. I searched the vanity, just in case he was adding another hiding place, though that would have been a poor choice, anything hidden there would be easy to notice. The bottles of hand lotion and shampoo, hydrogen peroxide, Band-Aids, they all looked so innocent, spilling against each other in the small space beneath the sink. I opened the medicine cabinet again and counted the antabuse tablets. I took two out of the bottle and put them in my pocket. I felt armed.

My father worked first shift at the shipyard, which meant he left for work about six-thirty in the morning and he'd get home around four. My mother left for work at eight-thirty and got home in time for supper. That gave me plenty of time during the day to carry out a search. I could find ways to keep Grace busy, or I could make a game out of it, set up a scavenger hunt for her and that way I could search while I set out the clues for Grace to find. She loved that game, it would be easy. I felt good, as though everything was going to be fine. There's something about having a plan of action that puts a person at ease, like little kids preparing for a nuclear attack by learning to throw themselves under a desk really fast. Hey kids! If you can duck and cover, why worry?

I followed the plan the next few days. I searched early in the mornings before Grace got up and on the mornings she was up early,

I found ways to poke around the house without letting her notice, though I probably could have dispensed with the drama, she wouldn't have known what I was doing if I turned every closet inside out. Reality had a very hard time sneaking up on Grace and that made my life easier. The rest of the week went by and everything was normal. I hadn't found bourbon anywhere and every morning there was one less pill in the bottle. I started to relax, even started feeling a little stupid about getting myself worked up over nothing.

And then Friday night there was a pill in the trash can. And Saturday morning there was a brand new can of oil on the workbench in the garage. This is how it starts, the making of a bomb. You gather all the pieces - the glass, the wires, the bits of metal that will explode into the air and shred everyone that stands in the way; the poison gas that will suffocate us, or set us on fire. You put the pieces together in secret. You set it off.

Step one, stop taking medication. Step two, hide alcohol. And we could only sit and wait until the blast had blown over and then look around to see what was still standing.

Sunday was the day of Willie's funeral. It was to be an afternoon service after the eleven o'clock mass. And here I stood in the garage, in the dark because the windows were dirty and barely any light could get through, staring at the small can of oil. It was one of those flat cans with the opening on the top, a little bit like a flask. A week ago we were at the beach. A week ago Willie was alive and I barely thought about him. How is it, I wondered, that a week ago we couldn't see any of this coming. Why don't we get any warning?

The oil can had been opened and the hinges on one of the doors was wet and greasy. This was another sign of preparation, the focused attention on just one door, despite the fact that all the hinges were rusted. I opened the door, which swung easily and silently. There were no bottles in there, at least not yet. I closed the door, latched it again, so he wouldn't be able to tell I was there.

I went in the house and found Celeste in the kitchen.

"Hey Celeste," I said. I tried to sound chipper, but my voice was a little too loud, unnaturally loud and happy.

"Cripes sake Claire!" she shrieked. She jerked the full glass of milk she was holding in one hand and sloshed milk onto the table, Mrs. Bergeron style. "You scared the bejeezus out of me!" She held her other hand against her chest like she was trying to hold her heart in. "What are you doing up so early anyway?" She soaked the milk up with the section of the newspaper she was reading.

"Calm down already, geez, it's my kitchen." I took a seat at the table and poured a bowl of cereal. She took a few breaths of air and blew them out slowly. Her eyes were closed and she held her hands up, middle finger and thumbs pressed together.

"What's that supposed to be?" I asked her. "Is that some Zen thing?"

"Are you going to Willie's funeral?" she asked, her eyes still closed, fingers still pressed together. "It's at one, I think. I'm going, we need to sit together. This is a very relaxing pose, by the way. You should try it. You look like a train wreck."

"I can't go," I told her. "My mother doesn't want Grace there and I have to stay home with her."

"But that's not fair!" she said. Her eyes snapped open and she slammed her hands on the table, all that Zen magic lost in an instant. "You should be there. We were all friends. He'd want you there!"

She looked stricken, like she really believed Willie would know I wasn't there and that I'd be hurting his feelings if I didn't attend his funeral.

"There's nothing I can do about it." My eyes teared up looking at her, thinking about Willie. "You know how my mother is."

"My brothers are going, both of them, and they're younger than Grace!"

She was angry, and she was right to be angry. And poor Willie, he would have been hurt. It's true. I could almost see him standing next to Celeste, his hand on her shoulder, trying to calm her down. *Crissake Celeste, it's not the end of the world. I don't care about a funeral.* But his face, his eyes mostly, would say something else. His face would tell me that he would like me to be there. He'd want to see me cry.

Ordinarily, I would have been outraged, too. I would have been furious at my mother for making me stay home and miss the funeral.

But the truth was I needed to stay home. I needed to stay home so I could figure out my plan.

"Tell me all about it when you get back," I told Celeste. "I'll be at the Menard's house afterward."

There was going to be a gathering at Mr. Menard's right after the burial, one final event before we could put Willie to rest. My mother said it was all right for Grace to attend that.

"It won't be the same," Celeste said. "Not at all." She looked at me, confused. I knew she wasn't going to understand why I was giving in to my mother so easily. And I wasn't going to explain it to her. I wasn't going to tell her my plan, still forming in my head, about how I was going to take the antabuse tablets I had stolen, grind them up, and pour the powder into an envelope, the way a criminal in an Agatha Christie novel might store poison. That I had to figure out when and where to use the powder. That I had to search for bottles he may have purchased but not stored in the garage yet. That I would have to empty them, if I dared. Cut the wires. I had to cut the wires.

She knows.

What do you mean by that?

She searches. She searches the house.

You're being ridiculous.

She does it every time. She looks for your hiding places.

Stop it.

Why do you ruin everything?

My father heads down the stairs, I can hear the carpeted steps groan as he passes each one. Then the cellar door opens and the sound of his footsteps disappears. It is late fall, and he is hiding his bottles in the old dresser that has been stored in the basement for years. We are supposed to give it to charity, but we never have. It is too cold at night to sit in the yard behind the garage and drink, so he goes downstairs. Fair weather drinking places. Cold weather drinking places.

I do search the house, it's true, but it is a useless venture. I am useless. I am afraid to pour his whiskey out. Afraid to touch the bottles the way I'm afraid to touch a live fish that is flopping on the ground, dying and desperate. My hands reach for the glass bottles, but I always pull back.

I try very hard to sleep so I won't be awake to hear when he comes back up the stairs. But it is hours later and I am still awake when he comes back up from the cellar. I can hear him stumble and he falls against the wall. He makes the house shudder. My mother runs down the stairs and I wish she would stay where she is. She will make it worse. She always makes it worse. She will tell him to leave, to just get out and leave us all alone. When he laughs at her, she will tell him she wants to kill him and he will laugh again and tell her he wishes she would try.

The noise from downstairs gets loud and Grace wakes up. She crawls into my bed and tells me she had a nightmare and that even though she's awake, she is still having it. She is dreaming that the house has turned into a monster and we are all trapped inside. She has this dream often and I know it's because four year olds can't interpret things. Or maybe, as I think about it, I realize they can. Because we really are trapped inside *something.*

Tell me a story, she says. I want you to tell me a story. She curls her-
self up into a ball, her head is touching her knees and she is almost a
perfect circle.

I tell her the story of the bird that lives in a cave, a rotted bird, almost
dead, that has no feathers. It is flightless. It hides in a cave because it is
ashamed. One night, the moon shines so brightly, the white light reaches
the back of the cave where the naked bird sits, and shines on her brightly.
A small bird, pretty in a coat of dark blue feathers, has been following the
moonlight, and she flies into the cave. She is surprised to find the scowl-
ing, ugly bird. The blue bird is full of pity and would help if she could, but
she is old and has only a thimbleful of magic left in her. I will give you all I
have left, she tells the featherless bird, and hands her two small eggs.
Hatch these eggs. Whatever lives will help you. The ugly bird begins to
speak, to complain that she can't hatch these eggs, she has no feathers to
keep them warm, but the small bird disappears. The ugly bird gathers the
eggs to her, and presses them against her cold chest.

In the morning, she ventures outside into the sunshine. She wants to
warm her eggs. The bright sun sears her open eyes, and blinds her. With-
out seeing, she places the eggs on the ground and lets the sun warm them
all day. Just as night falls, they crack open, one at a time, and when the
ugly bird realizes that they are alive, she feels a happiness unknown to her
before. She is not happy because she believes they might save her, she is
just happy to know they are alive. She gathers the little birds to her, hold-
ing them in her bony wings like they are one. She breathes in their
warmth.

I know that I should end the story here, that there is a moral I have
been moving toward, the lesson that tells you once you are loved, you are
saved. But such an ending would upset Grace, she wants everything to be
perfect. For Grace, salvation lies in beauty. So I continue past where the
story really ends and give her the predictable ending, just this once.

The young birds are pretty, I tell her, they look like the magic bird who
delivered them. They are kind, like she was. The first small bird reaches
out a dark blue wing and brushes the bird's eyes, and she is no longer
blind. The second spreads its wings wide and embraces the ugly bird, and
she begins to sprout feathers, midnight blue, like the young ones. As soon

as the moon is at its highest point in the sky, she is covered in feathers and able to fly. They leap together into the night air and for the first time, the flightless bird soars.

Grace wants to know where they fly off to, and whether they will ever return to the cave, and won't she be homesick, even if she never liked the cave. But I tell her that is where the story ends. She should know the bird by now, she should be able to think like the bird. I will not make it any nicer for her, or she'll grow up expecting everything ends in perfection.

The house has quieted down and I wonder if I will find my father asleep on the couch in the morning and whether my mother will have to call Mr. Bergeron and tell him that he's sick and can't work. But from the darkness of my room I can make out a shadow in the doorway, tall and wide enough to fill the space almost completely. My father tells me that was a nice story, his voice a strong whisper. He walks across the room and bends over the bed, holding onto the headboard because he is unsteady, and kisses us both on the forehead and tells us goodnight and that we should be happy, everything is going to be all right. He tells us we are perfect.

CHAPTER Ten

T he cars returned slowly to the neighborhood, one behind the other, as though no one had noticed that a hearse was no longer leading them. They were sheep who had lost their shepherd but whose path was so embedded in their brains, they had no need for him. Grace and I were on the porch, playing a game of checkers, or rather, hundreds of games of checkers since it took me about three seconds per game to beat her.

"C'mon Grace," I said, "you're not even trying. This is so boring." I could have let her win, but I didn't like to patronize her.

Grace was in a bad mood, partly because she was a sore loser, and partly because she was hungry. I hadn't bothered to fix lunch since we were going to be eating after Willie's service was over. It took much longer than I thought it would, the funeral mass and burial. I had never been to one, so I didn't know.

My parents came up the porch steps together and we all just looked at each other, none of us knowing how to start a conversation after a funeral. It wasn't like someone coming home from the fair where you could ask if it was fun. My father broke the silence by asking me if I'd made the potato salad.

"Yup," I said, and my voice sounded fake to my ears, an uplifting lilt with no truth behind it.

"You did?" he asked. He sounded skeptical. "Did you make it like I said? Did a fine dice on the onion and the pickle? Potatoes not too mushy?" When I assured him I had done it right, he said, "Good job. Let's head over. This has been a long day and I'd like to get home and relax a little."

The Bergerons and Celeste's family were already crowded together at the foot of Mr. Menard's driveway by the time we made it to the house. We joined them and waited for the Gerards, who were a short distance behind us. Then we all just stood there while the adults discussed proper protocol for entering the bereaved's home after a funeral and burial. No one really knew, not even Mr. Gerard. Not even my father, who could usually be relied on in moments like these. He stood there like someone who'd just flown in from another country, completely lost. Mr. Bergeron concentrated on his hand, which was still encased in a white bandage, so clean and fresh, it looked like new fallen snow. Mrs. Bergeron was taking good care of him, evidently.

"How's the hand Emile?" Mr. Gerard asked him, "You doing all right?"

"Oh, can't complain," Mr. Bergeron told him. "Can't complain. Didn't lose quite two fingers this time, so that's good."

"And there won't be a next time, believe you me," Mrs. Bergeron interjected. "No sir. He's getting one of those little push mowers, one with no engine on it."

"She's making me go all old fashioned," Mr. Bergeron said. "It's gonna take me a day and a half if I ever want to get my lawn done."

Everyone guffawed politely then looked down and scraped the driveway with the bottom of their shoes. Uncertainty settled back down over us. My father was casting his eyes over the bowls of food everyone was holding and I knew he was thinking the same thing I was, that every dish had mayonnaise in it and if we didn't get inside soon, it would turn and we'd all poison ourselves.

"What's wrong with you people?" A voiced bellowed from across the street and Uncle Romeo charged up the driveway. "You look like a bunch of nuns standing outside a strip club." It wasn't often anyone looked relieved when Uncle Romeo showed up, but we couldn't have been any happier at that moment. Finally, a leader. He slapped my father on the shoulder, nodded to my mother and then led the way into the house like Moses just after parting the Red Sea, flush with invincibility.

I wondered how invincible he'd feel if he'd known the role he played in this tragedy. If he'd known that the only reason my father had rushed to get the branch taken down was so Uncle Romeo wouldn't be the one to do it. I wondered how lost and guilty he'd feel if he'd known Willie had taken his place on the roof, because we didn't trust him to do it and that Willie died for him. You could look at it that way. You could imagine that Uncle Romeo had been saved. He was saved from the danger and saved from the guilt. Guilt was a crown of thorns and Uncle Romeo had no idea how lucky he was that he didn't have to wear it. My father was wearing it, I could tell by the look on his face when he left for the funeral, eyes without focus, shoulders drooping and back bent from muscles too loose and weak to hold him upright. His silence. The resounding silence that was like cymbals crashing in my head.

I had performed my search routine as usual that morning, half afraid to find a bottle because I didn't know if I'd have the nerve to pour it out. I never had before, not till now. I noticed two new bottles of hydrogen peroxide under the sink, value-sized, the kind they sold at Fortin's drugstore. Two huge bottles. That was a lot of peroxide. My father had poured the peroxide out of the bottles and filled them with whiskey. I was sure it was whiskey, a particular brand, because he always bought the same kind that had a sickening, syrupy smell.

The liquid was golden amber against the white of the sink as I turned the bottles, one by one, upside down and emptied them. I poured out both bottles before I thought about what I was doing, because that's really the only way to get things done. Don't worry about what you're doing. Don't dwell on it, like when you jump off a dock into cold lake water. You'll stand on the dock all day if you think about how cold the water is, how dark it will be the whole time you're submerged, how you'll have to hold your breath. No, you can't think, or you'll never do it. And after you jump, well, there's no stopping in midair.

That's how I emptied the bottles. As the last of the dark liquid twisted like a whirlpool down the drain, I came to and realized what I was doing, and I wanted to undo it. I wanted it all back safely in the dark brown peroxide bottles. I wanted the bottles to remain undiscovered. But it was too late. The amber liquid was gone, running down the bathroom drain, into the pipes that ran through the walls of the house, to the conduits that ran underground. I filled the empty bottles with water and put them back under the sink, where I had found them. I didn't know what was going to happen when he found out.

"Claire!" Uncle Romeo was shouting at me. "You got a wooden leg? C'mon."

I must have looked ill, because when I got to the top of the steps, he put his arm around my shoulders and gave me an awkward hug. "Don't worry about anything," he said, "you leave everything to me."

The Menard's house was dark inside. I don't think this was because Mr. Menard was trying to create a somber mood, I'm pretty sure their house was always dark inside. They were one of these families that always kept the shades drawn, even during the day. I always imagined the inside of their house must be stifling, and it was. Heavy with years of cigarette smoke and dust that had no choice but to hang in the air, no fresh breeze to stir it around, ever. It almost had a personality, a smoke ghost curling around you, trying to make you feel at home.

Mr. Menard was sitting in a recliner in the living room, already surrounded by plates of the food we had brought in. He wasn't eating anything. He just sat there staring at the blank screen on the television set as though he were watching Gunsmoke, Willie's favorite show. I wondered if he was imagining Willie sitting near him in the other recliner, the two of them watching their favorite program together, with the house blissfully empty of other people. He looked up when I stepped into the living room. He didn't smile, but he nodded slightly as he caught my eye. At this sign of life, people started talking to him, asking if he needed anything, did he want something to drink? Did he have enough to eat?

"Claire," he said, looking at me as though I were the only other person in the room. "Can you sit down here for a minute?"

He leaned over a coffee table cluttered with magazines, a few books, and about a hundred plates of food. He made a little room at the edge of the coffee table, stacking the plates on top of one another, not paying any attention to the food that was on them. Some of the silverware fell off the table and the pieces made two distinct sounds at once, a clattering chime as they hit together and a thudding silence as they landed on the carpet. Mr. Menard reached to pick them up and then he just held them in his hands. I felt angry at that moment. Angry at all these stupid neighbors who insisted on crowding into this man's house, to make sure he knew how sorry they all were, as though that was the most important task they could think of doing. All this food, all this murmuring and sniffling, it was rules and tradition. And now he had to sit there, holding knives and forks in his hands because he was at a loss and that put him at their mercy.

I walked across the room and sat at the end of the coffee table. "Hi Mr. Menard," I said, too softly. I wasn't sure he heard me. "How are you doing?" I raised my voice so it could plow through the heavy air and reach him.

"Oh. I'll be all right. Not to worry. Don't worry about me." I had no idea about grief, and I was afraid he was about to have a breakdown because the way he spoke was so disturbing, so unnatural. But then he stopped and was silent for a second. "I wanted to ask you," he said, pausing as I shifted on the edge of the table. "I want to know how it happened. I want to know, did he say anything?"

The question brought me back to the morning of the accident, and I caught my breath at the speed of it. I didn't want to talk about what happened because then I would have to think about it again, but Mr. Menard looked desperate. So I told him about that day, what the weather was like, how Willie offered to fix some things in the house, like the sagging wood in the porch steps, the screen door that slammed so hard. How he struggled with the ladder and when I told him to be careful, he said he was ok, that the ladder wasn't heavy, just awkward.

"Just awkward," Mr. Menard said, and nodded his head as though he understood what Willie had meant. "That ladder is awkward, he's right. All ladders are. Not meant to be carried, no. No they're not. Easier if you move it with two people. We always moved it together."

I hesitated before I continued because I didn't know how long he was going to go on talking about the ladder and I didn't want to interrupt him. Somehow, it felt as though he needed to contemplate the ladder, the last thing Willie had held onto. The thing that had ultimately killed him. I told Mr. Menard how Grace and I played with the kitten in the yard while Willie got out the chainsaw. How he climbed the ladder and I heard him swear and when I looked up, it was just as he was clinging to the roof overhang, and then how everything fell, one at a time. The chainsaw, the ladder, and then Willie.

"I should have been there, I shouldn't have let him set up alone." He took a handkerchief out of his pocket and wiped his eyes. "He was still just a kid. Just a kid." And then he said to me, "I'm sorry. I'm sorry you had to see that. That must have been hard for you." He shook his head and told me again he couldn't be sorrier for me.

If he hadn't taken pity on me, I might have made it through the whole gathering without losing my composure, which for some reason felt like an important thing to hold onto. But there's something about a man forgetting, even for a moment, the blow that cut his life in half, and recognizing how that same blow cut something out of you, too. So we sat there for a few minutes, feeling really sorry for each other, and then I started crying. I tried to act like I wasn't, like my eyes were just itchy from all the cigarette smoke in the room, and I tried to cough away the gasping sobs I could feel rising up from my chest. You always sound so much worse when you try not to cry, like some big animal's got you by the throat and is trying to crawl inside. Better to give in and just get it over with. Mr. Menard was still holding two fistfuls of silverware when he leaned forward and put his arms around my shoulders, knives and forks pressed against the side of my head as he hugged me.

It was about an eternity later when Mr. Menard stood up, his eyes dimmed and lifeless, the last of whatever was living inside of him running down his face.

But he had enough left to wave one hand, still clutching the silverware, in the direction of my father. He looked like he wanted to say something but couldn't find the words. So he didn't say anything, instead he just shook the glittering mass of silver in the air before letting it all fall to the floor where the pieces lay scattered, looking bright and gleaming against the dark color of the rug. He turned and walked to the door of his bedroom. He opened it, stepped inside and closed it behind him, shutting us out.

The noise in the room evaporated for a long, uncomfortable moment.

"What did he mean by that?" my father asked. "Why'd he do that?" His voice was loud, I could feel the echo of it in my bones.

Uncle Romeo told him to never mind. "People do crazy things at times like these. He didn't mean anything by it. Just a nervous reaction."

The men all lit cigarettes, because that's what they did when they didn't want to talk. For a few seconds it was silent except for the clicking of lighters and the intake of smoky breaths. My father told me to head into the kitchen, to go see if my mother needed any help. I did as I was told. I was glad to, my eyes were stinging from the cigarette smoke and it was hard to breathe.

CHAPTER Eleven

Bad things happen in threes, that's what I'm worried about."

All the mothers were in the kitchen. It was a small kitchen, but bright, probably the only sunny room in the house. It wasn't as smoky in here since only Celeste's mother was smoking, and she was leaning toward an open window and blowing cigarette smoke through the screen. As the smoke broke apart through the mesh, she watched it and as it disappeared, she said it again, "Bad things happen in threes, you all know that, right?"

The other women were doing their best to ignore her, especially my mother. She had her back to the window and pretended to be really busy putting some olives onto a plate. Mrs. Gerard handed her a bowl, telling her that might be better to use, since otherwise the olives might end up rolling all over the floor. My mother gave her a weak smile and said thanks. But when she tried pouring the olives from the plate to the bowl, most of them rolled off the plate anyway and started bouncing off the table and onto the floor. More olives were lost that way than if she'd just tried serving them off the plate to begin with. Olives aren't perfectly round, so they don't roll all that well and they sort of moved around like the little Weebles Grace still played with. They were easy to pick up. Celeste and I picked them all up off the floor and I threw them in the trashcan. Mrs. Gerard shook her head like she was witnessing a public execution and murmured softly, "Pity to waste such good food."

That was the first moment I ever hated anybody.

"It's just some olives," I said sharply, speaking out loud before giving it any thought. Grace and Celeste looked at me. I could tell they weren't breathing. My mother gave me one of her sharp looks and I gave her the same look back because, for a brief moment, I didn't care. Not for that one pinprick of time, that first grain of sand that falls through an hourglass, free and alone until the hour's worth of sand behind it begins its smothering free-fall. I didn't care about anything except the anger I had for Mrs. Gerard and her clumsy olive eulogy.

"Well! I never!" she said. She had a pointy face, I never thought she was pretty, but now her face seemed to take on the contours of a witch. An ugly one, the kind you'd find in one of my mother's fairy tales.

"You never what?" my mother asked, turning slowly in Mrs. Gerard's direction. There was a tone to her voice I hadn't heard before, harsher than anything she'd ever used against me. "Never known a child who watched someone die? Never had a tragedy yourself? Never dropped anything?" Her voice rose and her accent thickened, but we could still understand her pretty well. "You think she should worry about olives?" My mother slammed the plate down on the table and it cracked in half, a perfect straight line right down the middle.

Mrs. Gerard was stunned. We all were. There was electricity in the air, it felt as though a current connected us and none of us could move or speak until it was grounded.

"I just meant I never knew Claire to speak to an adult that way, that's all." Mrs. Gerard looked small and her voice sounded distant. Her gaze flickered between my mother and me, and for a moment I thought she was going to apologize.

"Let's all take a deep breath," Mrs. Cartier said brightly. She held her hands up in the air, fingers pressed together like Celeste had been doing lately. "We need to change the energy in this room!"

Making people feel bad was her area of expertise and Celeste's mother didn't like other people honing in on her territory. She got everybody to calm down with her by making us all breathe into our diaphragms and saying 'Om' a couple of times.

"So, as I was saying," she continued once she had gotten her audience back, at least partially. We all kept looking at my mother and Mrs. Gerard, wondering if they were done with each other or if we could expect another round. "Bad things happen in threes. What could possibly happen next do you think? First poor Mr. Bergeron with his hand, then poor Willie. I just can't imagine, not at all." She lit another cigarette and blew a smoke ring out the window.

I could tell by the look on Celeste's face that she'd had about enough of her mother. We both were a little unnerved, so I started putting food on my plate and told her to come with me, to come sit outside. I wanted to leave, to get outside where there was thin, clear air. We piled our plates so we wouldn't have to come back and left through the back door.

We didn't say much as we walked out to the backyard. It looked the same as it had the last time we were out here, but it felt like another world. I missed Willie and I could tell Celeste did too. She looked lost and she started to sag a little bit. I had to tell her to hold her plate straight because all her food was about to slide off.

We had the choice of sitting at the picnic table that was parked directly under an oak tree or at the table where we last sat with Willie, just a few days earlier. We gravitated toward the picnic table but it was covered with lichen and acorns. Years of harsh weather had gouged crevasses in the wood, and tiny oak trees were sprouting from the table top, forming a grove of miniature trees. We stood there a few moments, trying to decide whether it was too much work to clear off a space for us to sit. An acorn popped off one of the giant branches and danced around on the ground, and then another bounced off the picnic table and took a swan dive onto the green grass. Celeste said she wouldn't be able to relax if she kept worrying that acorns were going to rain down on her, so we sat at the white metal table, veined with rust, the chairs unmoved since we were last there.

Willie's chair, the one between us, stayed empty. We just sat there, both of us trying to decide what to look at, the red pool of water, our plates, each other. I couldn't think of anything to say, or anything that wouldn't sound stupid and contrived. But it felt wrong, somehow, to sit there and not acknowledge the last time we were there.

"Celeste, where's my cat?" Grace, blind to the mini wake we were holding, dropped herself into Willie's empty chair and set her plate on the table next to mine. She never ate more than a tablespoon of food, but it looked like a starving animal had loaded her plate.

"Grace, are you even going to eat any of that?" Sometimes it got on my nerves, how she always wanted to be like everyone else, how she'd do things like overload her plate because all the other kids did and then she'd proceed to eat a slice of pickle and a molecule of ham.

"That is just ridiculous. Talk about a waste of food," I said.

"Such a pity," Celeste said, and she gave a pretty good impersonation of Mrs. Gerard mourning a handful of ruined olives.

"I never!" Grace finished, waving her finger in the air in a slight over dramatization, and that was that. We were done with this day, done with the end of Willie. The better part of our grief was gone, seeped into the earth like a wave spread thin across the beach, disappearing before the tide is able to pull it back. That created a new grief all its own of course, that specter of loss that would shadow us from that point on, but one that was light, so light it was practically weightless, one we could live with. And being able to live with it that was sad to me. I wondered what Willie would think of that. *Don't worry about it Claire, no big deal.* His voice was somewhere in my head. *Get off it, I didn't expect you to die with me!*

And so we ate. There was really nothing else to do. Even long after we were full, we kept eating. Grace cleared almost half her plate and I started to worry that she was overdoing it since I'd never seen her eat that much all at once.

"I'm about to barf," Celeste announced.

"Me too," Grace said and she pushed her plate across the table. She got up and walked to the edge of the pond, holding her stomach like she really was going to lose it. When she leaned over, I thought she was ready to throw up, but she was just looking into the water's edge. "Is there anything living in there?" she asked. She bent low and ran her fingers across the water. "Can we feed some fish?"

Only Grace would ask something like that. Thick ropes of red algae stretched along the edge of the pond. If you threw a rock or a stick into it, the algae would break apart and drift like smoke across the top of the water. It would come apart even more when it reached an auto hood or the top of the washing machine that had been there for about a year at that point, not rusted yet, still shiny enough for the sun to reflect off the chrome.

"Nothing in there but piranhas," Uncle Romeo called out. "Vicious ones, so you better watch those fingers. You'll turn out like Mr. Bergeron." Uncle Romeo and my father, along with everyone else who had been in the living room, had come outside to stand in the backyard under the long shade of the oak tree. Grace let out a scream and flung herself away from the edge of the pond like some swamp creature had just emerged. You couldn't really say things like that to Grace. She believed everything. But it was good for a little comic relief and we all got a mild laugh out of it.

Only my father kept on laughing. After everyone else had tapered off, he kept laughing at her. "Isn't she amazing?" he asked. "Amazing Grace, that's my little girl. Amazing Grace!" And he held his sides, embracing himself, as though the laughter was too much.

Mr. Bergeron and Mr. Gerard started laughing again, even after they'd stopped, just so it wouldn't seem too awkward, but there is nothing more disheartening than fake laughter, so it didn't help. It only made everything more absurd. My father had been drinking. Somehow he had managed to stash a bottle somewhere, under the front seat of the car most likely. He had dug it out when no one was looking, maybe after Mr. Menard threw the silverware on the floor. If he drank it fast enough, it hit him hard and quick.

Uncle Romeo stood next to my father, solemn. As crazy as he could be, I never saw him with a smile on his face when my father was drinking. He stopped his wild stories, he lost his loud voice. It dried him up, this lifetime spent alongside a bloodsucker. You wouldn't think anyone could make a funeral gathering worse than it naturally is, but here was living proof. Leave it to my father and his whiskey.

Mr. Bergeron suggested a game of horseshoes. It was kind of him, I know he said that because the game was set up off to the side of the house and he wanted to get my father away from us and the other little kids that had come outside. Tossing iron horseshoes around was probably not the best idea at that moment, but I appreciated the gesture.

"Sounds like fun!" my father shouted, too loud. Too happy. He smiled at his grim-faced neighbors, his soul already bartered for whiskey, drowning and almost out of sight now, unable to realize no one was playing along. A soulless man is deaf and blind. In a few minutes, we could hear the clanking of horseshoes and rising shouts of praise followed by the dull thuds of near misses and groans of disappointment. "Careful Frank!" someone called out, and I cringed.

I never knew what to say when this happened. I had no idea what to do. It was better if my father's drinking was evident only in the house, where there wasn't a whole neighborhood, my whole world really, standing there gawking like they were waiting for a skydiver to hit the ground at a thousand miles an hour.

"I'm not allowed to play horseshoes." Peter, one of Celeste's little brothers, was standing in front of me, his typical grave expression chiseled onto his face. "Celeste got hit in the head when she was little, so we can't play. We're not allowed."

Ordinarily, I would have said something like 'Well, that explains a lot', but I didn't have it in me. Everything around me seemed old and faded, and I felt as though I was fading right along with it. I knew that even if I tried to say something, it would come out in a whisper so quiet I didn't think anyone would hear me.

The game of horseshoes continued, the clang of metal against the post followed by the heavy thud of the shoes that missed, men's voices rising like and falling with the cadence of their game.

Once, when I was little, before Grace was even born, there was a rain shower in our neighborhood. It rained on the Menard's house and all the houses on the far end of the street, while my house and all the neighbors near us stayed dry. I can remember standing at the end of my driveway looking down the street to where the rain was falling. It was like a curtain, the falling rain, so heavy and dark it hid all but the shapes of the other houses. But it stayed dry and bright where I was standing. Neighbors came out of their houses one by one, awed by the sight. "It's a miracle!" everyone was saying. "Go on Claire, go play in it." And it was fun, I remember. It was fun to hold hands with Celeste, one of us in the rain, one of us in the sun. We raced each other back and forth, zigzagging in and out of the heavy rainstorm, breathless at this ability to stand in the dead end of a storm.

It did make me believe in miracles, that rain shower, I will admit that. But as miracles go, it was worthless. And that's why I didn't pray for a miracle that day.

CHAPTER Twelve

At least my father wasn't the only one who had trouble walking home later that night. Mr. Bergeron had mixed beer with his pain pills and he started enjoying the game of horseshoes as much as my father. He had to throw with his left hand and it quickly became a contact sport, leaving the other players no choice but to hop out of the way once he got swinging. Uncle Romeo took them both of them home, letting them lean on each other as they did a weaving dance up the street. Mrs. Bergeron had gone on ahead of them, apologizing to the other mothers about not helping to clean up, but they told her not to worry, they'd clear the kitchen. She marched ahead of my father and Mr. Bergeron, her green tent dress flowing behind her. From behind, she looked queenly. But her face had been set hard when she left.

Celeste and I started a game of kick the can with the rest of the kids, which continued long after the street lights came on. It was a full moon that night and a full moon always made the game harder to play since it was more difficult to hide. We used the whole neighborhood as a playground and I ran by my house several times, hovering outside the open windows to listen, but I couldn't hear anything. I didn't know if that was good or bad.

I wanted to go inside and check on things, sort of the way a person will run into a burning building to see what can be saved. It's a bad idea. I read once that there is something about fire that attracts a person, that there is something innate in us that pulls a person within inches of burning. We're a little like moths that way, only not quite as stupid. So I didn't go in, I just lurked near the open windows. Besides, after the words my mother had thrown at Mrs. Gerard, I had grounds to believe that she might do something, confront my father maybe, or persuade him somehow to stop now before it all got out of hand. I wasn't too hopeful about it, but it gave me a reason to stay outside a

little longer, running as fast as I could through my neighbors' back-
yards, the cascading moonlight acting as my ally in finding all the
little kids who thought a narrow birch tree made a good hiding place.

When the game was over, Grace and I walked home. We were
sticky with sweat and bug spray and itchy with mosquito bites because Maine mosquitoes, big as bats with similar radar, could always
find the one microscopic spot on your skin that you left unprotected.
Halfway up the driveway we had to stop so I could scratch her back
where she had gotten bites though her t-shirt. "I hate getting bug
bites on my back," she said.

"I know," I agreed. "They're so hard to get to. But that's still better
than breathing one in through your nose. Remember that happened
to you one time?"

Grace laughed at that and said she remembered, that it was disgusting how she breathed a mosquito in straight past her sinuses
directly into her throat and she almost choked on it. "I ended up swal-
lowing it, it was so gross."

"It was hilarious. You're always good for a laugh, ever notice that?
You'll have a complex about it one day."

"What's a complex?"

We climbed the steps to the porch, sinking slightly on the broken
board and I was forced, once again, to think of Willie. I held the door
open for Grace and stepped inside right behind her, shutting and
locking the door behind me.

"Girls, go up and get ready for bed." My mother was standing in
the middle of the living room and I knew she had been waiting for us,
and yet she looked startled when we opened the door. My father was
sitting on the couch, his guitar across his lap. We had gotten him a
new guitar a few years earlier because he'd been playing the same old
guitar since he was a kid. He hadn't gotten any better at it, he still only knew about three chords but that was enough to get by. He could
sing pretty much every song he knew using just those three chords,
or he thought he could anyway. It was embarrassing, really, but he
had so much fun with it, we never said anything. He liked to make up
songs about Grace, sung somewhat to the tune of 'Amazing Grace'.
He could always make it funny, but not when it sounded slurry and

dull-witted.

"Hey, hey! Just wait a minute here, I got a little song for Grace. Just let me finish up tuning this here guitar." His voice was still too loud and now included a noticeable twang. For some reason, he thought all songs played on a guitar were automatically country and he sang his lyrics accordingly.

"It's late Frank, it's time for them to go upstairs."

"Don't be a spoil sport Marie. Just one song, one little song. Here we go girls." He cleared his throat.

It was that classic moment all kids hate, when your mother tells you to do one thing and your father says to do something else. We tried to follow both directives. We headed upstairs slowly, but paused often to turn and look at him to show him we were listening. Grace even nodded her head as though she were keeping time with his rhythm. He strummed a chord two or three times then paused briefly as he readjusted his fingers to change the sound. He sang a ridiculous tune that didn't rhyme, a stupid story of the little girl who leapt from the water's edge, afraid of something that turned out to be nothing at all, a girl afraid of the shadows of things. A careless girl, sticking her hands in opaque water, tempting the creatures below the surface. It went on and on.

If he wasn't drunk, he could have made something of it. It could have been some type of ballad, a thing he was good at. But coming from a drunk, it just sounded mean and scary. And there was Grace, bobbing her head like she was really enjoying herself, like she loved this sort of thing. Loved being ridiculed by a drunk. If he could have just stopped at some point, just ended with a loud, harsh scrape of the strings, a crescendo ending that would have signaled permission to go upstairs and get into bed. If only he didn't need to keep singing, all nonsense and meanness. If he could only ever have stopped before someone started crying.

We were more than half way up the stairs and we couldn't climb any higher because we would have been out of his sight. My mother remained in the middle of the living room, her arms folded across her chest, eyes pinned to the floor. He paused to rearrange his fingers on the strings and my mother used the opportunity to say it was enough.

"The girls have to get to bed Frank, it's late." She turned her face toward him and I could see she was crying. I couldn't hear it in her voice, it remained strong and unbroken, the way it sounded when she spoke to Mrs. Gerard, but tears rimmed her eyes and clung to her eyelashes the way rain will grab hold of a leaf and not drop to the ground until it gets too heavy.

"You don't like my song?" His face became a mask, the one he wore at this stage of drunkenness. A fake look of disappointment, like we had all gone out of our way to hurt him while he was doing his best to be good to us. This mask he'd wear said he didn't understand us. "Well all right then, if you don't want to hear my song, then don't listen. Go to bed if that's what you want to do, I'll sit here all by my lonesome." Even as he said this, he removed the guitar strap from around his neck and set the guitar into its case, so careful of it, it might have been made of glass, because in that moment it was the only thing he cared about.

My mother finally moved from her spot. She followed us up the stairs, silent in a pensive way that made me nervous. She directed Grace into the bathroom to take a shower and then went into her own room, but she didn't stay there. She came out every few minutes and walked the short landing between her room and mine, back and forth like a guard dog. It reminded me of the way she had turned on Mrs. Gerard, her hackles up, a scowl in her voice. She could stand up to my father too, but never for long.

I didn't realize how rigidly I was sitting on the end of my bed until she told me to relax. There must have been some reflection of her face in mine, because she came over and sat next to me on the bed. She pushed my hair behind my ear and took my hand. She hadn't been that close to me in a long time and I wondered why it had been so long. I couldn't remember when I had gotten too old to be treated like I was still a little kid.

"Are you excited about school starting in a few weeks?" She smiled and pushed my hair back again and I knew I was sitting there with my ears sticking out. Since I was about five, I did everything I could to make sure I never pushed my hair back, I never let myself get into that nervous habit off hooking my hair behind my ears because it made me look like Dumbo.

"Yeah, I guess." It was hard to listen to myself, and unnerving to hear my mother talk about school when we knew my father would be heading down to the cellar any minute to help himself to whatever he had hidden in the old dresser down there. Or out to the garage, where he'd hidden something, a bottle camouflaged against a backdrop of tools and oily rags. At some point, after we were in bed maybe, he would go into the bathroom and retrieve his peroxide bottles, try to take a drink. It would probably take him a few seconds to realize the tepid water tasted nothing like scotch whiskey.

"We'll go shopping for new school clothes next weekend, would you like that?" She was still making the motion of tucking my hair behind my ears, useless at this point since she had already raked all of it back.

"Sure," I said. We talked a little more about school clothes and what classes I might take and how much fun high school was going to be, all of it words to fill the air so that we didn't have to pay attention to anything else. Grace came out of the bathroom and my mother told me to go take a shower and then go to sleep, that it had been a long day and I had to get it behind me as quickly as I could.

The house was quiet when I turned off the light, Grace was already asleep. I stood at the window for a moment, it was wide open and the wind blew softly, inhaling and exhaling deep breaths like something asleep. The moon was low, so monstrous and fat, it was far too heavy to hang above the horizon. It filled my room with a blue light. I was amazed at how still the house was, how noiseless except for the breathing wind and the occasional sighing of the house joints that I could hear only at night.

There is a sense of bewilderment sometimes, at the soundless night. I imagined sailors coasting on a flat ocean surface, losing all fear that the water could ever rise against them, falling for the peaceful disguise until a sudden squall contradicts them. They are never taken completely by surprise, they're not fools, but they let themselves believe sometimes that the calmness of the ocean runs fathoms deep, that the sea is a sluggish, indolent creature that they don't need to fear.

It was quiet in our house until about midnight. My mother shook me awake, her hand clenched so hard around my shoulder I would see the mark of her fingers the next day. "Get Grace," she whispered. At first I didn't understand what she was saying. I just stared at her like I'd been mummified for the last thousand years. She had to shake me again and then she told me to wake up Grace and go over to the Bergeron's house. "Don't argue with me," she said, "just do it. Go."

It wasn't the first time we were sent over to the Bergeron's. When I was young, I never wanted to go because it was embarrassing and I didn't know what to say at two o'clock in the morning to neighbors I never spoke to in normal situations. But Mrs. Bergeron would pull me into her giant chest and tell me everything was fine, and then she'd pick up Grace and carry her inside. She'd make up the pull-out couch in the living room and settle us into it the way a grandmother might, with a lot of soft noises meant to comfort us and make us unafraid. Then she would send Mr. Bergeron over to our house, telling him to get my mother.

I pulled myself out of bed and got dressed in the dark. In the morning, I would realize that I couldn't have picked out anything uglier and I'd be humiliated in the light of day, but at that moment, I only thought about getting Grace out of the house. I grabbed one of her sundresses, it was thin cotton and sleeveless, so she was cold once she was out of bed and I had wrestled the dress over her head.

"We're just going to the Bergeron's house," I told her.

"Why?" she asked me. "Why do we have to go over there? What time is it?"

It should have been obvious, but maybe, like me, she didn't want to dwell on what was happening. "C'mon," I said, "follow me." She stumbled behind me, out the door and into the hallway.

My father was standing outside the bathroom door. He was holding the two brown bottles of peroxide upside down, shaking the water out of them, the carpet darkening as the water splattered down like the end of a storm. Once the bottles were empty he threw them hard against the wall. If they had been made of glass, they would have shattered into a million tiny shards and I would have worried about how I was going to get Grace across the hallway without getting fragments of glass in our feet since our shoes were in the closet downstairs. My mother came out of her room, probably to make sure Grace and I were leaving. She tried to ignore my father as she crossed in front of him to get to the stairs, motioning to me and Grace to follow her. When he saw her, he stepped into the hallway so he could pick up the bottles off the floor. He hurled them at her, one at a time. The first one missed and bounced off the wall and tumbled down the stairs. The second hit her in the back, but she kept going as though that one had missed her as well.

I pushed Grace ahead of me so she could go down the stairs first. She bent down to pick up the bottle that had hit my mother and I almost tripped over her. I had to grab the banister to keep from falling. She held it in her hands for a second and stared at it like she didn't know what to do with it now that she had picked it up. So she did what she usually did when she was confused and a little scared. She turned to my father and held the empty bottle out to him. "Here Dad," she said, "here you go." The strength went out of him, his head dropped and his mouth hung open. He reached out with his arm, limp and lifeless, and took the bottle from her.

"Thank you, Grace," he said, his voice barely perceptible.

I thought to myself how strange it was that we never lose our basic instincts. Grace always liked things neat, she didn't like chaos. It made me angry, a little bit, her having to pick up the stray bottle, like nothing going on around her was important. But it had a calming effect on my father, at least for a moment. He held the empty bottle in his hand like a man who'd been handed a gift he didn't deserve. It humbled him briefly and that gave us time to make it safely down the stairs and out onto the porch. My mother shut the front door behind us and before we were off the porch, I heard the bottle hit the door. I wondered if my mother had ducked or if his aim had been off.

CHAPTER Thirteen

God only gives us what we can handle, you know that Emile." The Bergerons were sitting at the kitchen table drinking the coffee that Mrs. Bergeron had started percolating on the stove as soon as we stepped into the house. She had that thing primed with coffee twenty-four hours a day, like a boy scout going for his coffee badge. It looked like Mr. Bergeron needed it. His face was a little gray and he kept burping, which made her look at him with slanted eyes.

"Who in his right mind ever said that?" Mr. Bergeron was asking. "Sounds like some politician up in Augusta trying to sell me on the idea of high fuel costs. It wasn't Jesus who said that, I've read the bible a hundred times if I've read it once."

"You've done no such thing Emile. Imagine you reading the bible a hundred times! Where's my rosary? I need to pray for you. And I'm pretty sure it was Jesus who did say it, and he'd know. Better than you anyway."

Grace and I were on the pullout couch in the living room, which was barely separated from the kitchen, and lying on my side, I could see them clearly. The doorway between the two rooms was so wide, the whole space was practically one room. Even though it was the middle of the night and they'd been asleep, Mrs. Bergeron had jumped into action as soon as I rang the doorbell. I felt bad, the way they knew just what to do. We were practically scheduled to be there. She had tossed the cushions off the couch and pulled out the mattress. It took her about two seconds to take sheets and pillows from the hall closet and make up the bed. She ushered us into it and I wondered why I had bothered to make sure we were both dressed before coming over, we weren't out of bed more than ten minutes. It just felt too strange to me, I suppose, to leave the house wearing a night gown.

"All I know," Mr. Bergeron said, "is these kids have a lot on their plate and I don't see the fairness of it."

Ordinarily, Mr. Bergeron would already have his shoes on and would be heading over to my house with two cups of coffee, one for him with cream and sugar and one for my father, nothing in it, just strong black coffee. Thick, slightly sludgy, if it had been percolating for a while, thin if it was fresh. He'd come back some time later, maybe half an hour, with my mother and no coffee cup. We had quite a collection of the Bergeron's coffee cups at our house. But tonight, he didn't head over. Mrs. Bergeron wouldn't let him, because of his hand. She thought he might do something to it and he didn't want him to end up back in the hospital. Maybe she had heard the screaming and crashing coming from my house and was afraid. Mr. Bergeron was all for going over, but he didn't put up too much of a fight. He must have thought her reasons were justified. Or maybe he was tired of always being the one to intervene.

They bickered a little more back and forth until they started repeating themselves. When Mrs. Bergeron accidentally slipped up and agreed with him, she abruptly cleared the table of their two coffee cups and poured the remaining coffee from the pot down the drain while Mr. Bergeron looked at her with a satisfied look on his face.

"We can agree on one thing - those girls need is a good night's sleep," she said, as though we weren't right there, a few feet away. I laid back on the bed and prepared for one uncomfortable night. The mattress on the pullout couch was so thin, I could feel the springs through it like I was laying directly on the coils. Grace squirmed around for a while, trying to find a spot that didn't dig into her. Mrs. Bergeron came over to the bed and tucked the blankets tightly under the mattress so I couldn't breathe. Mr. Bergeron stood leaning against the doorframe, his injured hand still in a sling. The bandages had been rewrapped and now it was possible to see where the missing fingers were. They told us good night, turned off the light, and left us.

Of course, we couldn't sleep. I loosened the blankets so we could move, and tried to get comfortable. Grace was crying, saying she wanted to go home and that the pillows smelled like mothballs. I told her everything was going to be all right, that we'd go home in the morning and everything would be fine. She could tell from my voice that I was lying. I might just as well have said the words. "I am lying. I am a liar." We're all liars, all the time.

"I want a story," she said, her voice sounded thick. I didn't say anything right away. It seemed odd, in that bed with the coils digging into us, in a house that was not our own, to want to hear a story. I just wanted silence, and time to figure out what I was going to do. Mr. Bergeron usually went over to my house when things got bad and we had to come over. He'd send my mother back and she'd spend a restless night in the recliner, the two of us taking turns being awake and worrying. Wondering what the next day would bring. But leave it to Grace to put all that out of her mind, she could drop herself into another world like a stone into a well.

It's what made her important, I guess. She was one of those people who could divide up life into different sections and live in them one at a time. Those are the people who keep the world spinning because they're the ones who never go crazy.

"All right," I said. "What do you want to hear? A real story or should I make something up?"

"A real story," she said. "Something true." As if there were such a thing. So I told her Snow White, the true tale of Snow White.

There was a Queen once, beautiful and stately and she reigned over a kingdom. She kept it nice. It was a safe place with enough food and work to keep everyone happy. Then one day this girl shows up out of nowhere. All the men immediately fall in love with her because she's so pretty. She's a simpleton, but they ignore that. Hardly any work gets done around the kingdom because all the men just sit around thinking about her. They are pining for this girl, and are only happy when they can catch a glimpse of her. They try to fake disinterest, but they can't fool the Queen. The Queen can see everything in her magic mirror, even inside hearts. She knows that all the work she's done to make the kingdom so wonderful is about to be undone, and so she has no choice but to get rid of this girl, Snow White. So the Queen orders her finest huntsman, which is really just another word for assassin, to kill her. Only he can't do it, and he's a paid killer. If he won't do it, the Queen knows she won't be able to get anyone to kill Snow White since everyone loves this girl so much. For no reason, I might add. So the Queen takes it upon herself to bring about Snow White's demise.

"But why?" Grace interrupts. "You're telling it wrong, the Queen is jealous, that's why she wants to kill Snow White."

But Snow White isn't a story about jealousy, I tell her. That's just the cover story. It's a story about a Queen who has given her life to this kingdom and all the people in it. The people will forget themselves, they'll lose direction. All they'll want to do is sit around and look at Snow White all day long. And you have to understand Grace, I tell her, the Queen has made sacrifices. Those dwarves, you know those dwarves that go mining all day, every day? Just how much gold and diamond can there be in one mine? The Queen keeps taking her gold and diamond jewelry and throwing it back into the mine so the dwarves have something to do. She loves these people and Snow White, well, she doesn't love the people. She never even takes the time to get to know them. It takes her months to even learn the dwarves' names, for crying out loud. And weren't their names pretty obvious? She only lives with them because they offer her a place to stay. And she's only going to stay until her Prince comes along. And then she'll go, leaving a bunch of useless mourners in her wake. The Queen is committed to the people. Snow White is just passing through.

Grace wasn't interested in hearing the rest, she insisted I was making it up and ruining a good story. I didn't press it. I told her she could believe whatever version she wanted, but that I was going to tell it like it is. "You sound like Mom," she said, and within a few minutes I could tell she was asleep and I don't know when, but at some point I was asleep, too.

Whether it was just in my head or if it was real, I wasn't sure at first. There was a noise like splinters hurled at a wall. For a hazy moment, I could see Snow White impaled against a white wall by a thousand shards of diamonds, bright spots of blood speckled across her dress. And then she was gone, and for a second it was quiet and I thought I had been dreaming.

The noise was coming from next door, from my house. At first I didn't do anything. Like any natural hero, I laid there, waiting for Mr. Bergeron to hear the sounds of fighting and get up and go over himself. I could pretend I was asleep and let the night pass away like it was any other. And then it was fifteen minutes later and the house was still dark and no one had moved.

I would have ignored it all if I could have. I had before. I could have buried my head in my pillow, curled up into a hard, impenetrable ball, feeling some sense of relief at being too young and weak to do anything. But now, I couldn't shake the guilt because I knew he was angry about the empty peroxide bottles. He'd have thought no one had ever been so clever, to hide whiskey in a pair of peroxide bottles. It was right up there with asking a cab driver to deliver a bottle to the house. My mother had thwarted my father before, warning the last cab driver who'd made a delivery that she'd bludgeon him with a baseball bat if he tried it again, and to go ahead and warn the other drivers because she'd do the same to them. Now he'd think she had found out his new trick seconds after he made the switch. The insult would be hard for him to take, not to mention the loss of his whiskey. And it was my fault.

So I got out of bed. I don't think I woke up Grace, although she could have been pretending. I got dressed, losing a few minutes as I tried to find my shoes in the dark before I remembered that I hadn't put them on.

I stepped out into the night, the air still a dark blue from the moon that continued to hang preternaturally close to the ground. I reached the porch steps and it was quiet except for the sound of my footsteps on the stairs. My mother was in the dining room, on her hands and knees picking broken pieces of things off the floor. She looked like a toy with weak batteries, slowly picking up a shard of a plate or cup, twisting slightly to drop it into a paper grocery bag on the floor beside her. She didn't look up as I came in. I didn't know what to do, I hadn't made any sort of plan, so I kneeled down next to her and started clearing the floor too.

"You're going to need a broom." My father stood in the entryway to the kitchen, his arms folded across his chest, a prison guard monitoring the inmates on work detail. He made it feel somehow natural, like we were all doing what was expected of us. We kept at it, my mother and I, picking up pieces of wrecked china with our fingers, careful to avoid cutting ourselves on the sharp edges. It was somehow soothing, this almost mechanical movement of hands and fingers from floor to paper bag. Over and over, a careful clearing of this sharp and jagged mess.

My father brought the broom over to where we were kneeling. He dropped it on the floor right next to me, and the broom handle sounded like the sudden, single explosion of fireworks. "I'll get the dustpan," he said as he turned back toward the kitchen. He walked as though he had lost faith that the floor was still beneath him, holding his arms out straight so he could touch the wall, and then the counter, for balance. He looked newly blind.

He returned a few minutes later with the dustpan and dropped that next to me as well. I don't think he was dropping things on the floor to scare us, I think he was past the point of being able to bend over without losing his balance. "Whatever you don't get, I can do in the morning." His voice was soft and slurred. And then he left, turning around slowly and heading toward the basement stairs on legs that didn't carry him straight, but rather in a sideways stumble, like a very tall crab. When we heard the basement door slam shut, my mother sat on the floor. I got up and started sweeping the rest of the mess because if I had stayed down on the floor beside her, I would have had to say something and my mind was vacant. I was just too tired to do anything but move the broom back and forth.

I cleaned the floor as well as I could, considering it was the middle of the night and my hands had started shaking. Sweat gathered into drops on my forehead and I felt nauseous. My mother looked at me and asked if I was all right, but she could tell I wasn't and all at once she was on her feet and rushing me into the kitchen. I vomited bile into the sink.

"You need to go to bed," she said to me. "Everything is going to be fine. You just need to sleep now." Despite the lifetime she had spent making sure I understood the dangers of the world, whenever push came to shove, she always fell back onto the same advice, just go to sleep. As though sleep were actually a place a person could go for refuge, like foreigners to an embassy. Lost souls to a sanctuary.

"OK," I said. I rinsed my mouth because it was burning and to-gether we left the house and started walking towards the Bergeron's. "You know," my mother said, "it isn't his fault, not really. This isn't your father."

I'd heard this before. Many times. He has a sickness and we have to be patient, let it run its course. No different from when I had a fe-ver and had to stay in bed.

"If we all stay out of his way, it will pass. It always does, you know it does." I wouldn't look at her, though I knew she was looking at me, looking to see if I was listening to her, wanting to see from my face whether I was able to understand what she was saying.

"Claire, don't interfere. Don't make it worse. Let's do what we al-ways do, it will be all right."

"OK," I said. But I wasn't sure I meant it, not yet anyway. We didn't say anything more as we walked in silence to the Bergeron's, the sound of our footsteps swallowed by the sound of crickets and their violin legs. They sounded disjointed, like each little cricket was tuning itself but never reaching a point where they were all ready to play together. They were an orchestra without a conductor. My mother and I, we ignored what we were both thinking, which was that dumping the peroxide bottles was a dangerous move. But the thought was so obvious, so present, that I felt berated anyway. I was shaky with guilt. Or maybe it was fatigue. It was the middle of the night and I didn't belong outside, not at this hour.

The Bergeron's house had stayed dark and silent. No one had woken up and noticed I was gone. I crawled back in bed, settling my-self down so that my shoulder blades rested between the coils, while my mother got a blanket out of the hall closet. She glided silently back into the living room and before she stretched out on the reclin-er, she tucked the blankets in around us, even tighter than Mrs. Bergeron had.

It is a Saturday night and I am allowed to stay home with Grace for the first time without a babysitter. I know my mother thinks I'm not quite old enough yet, but she is really hoping their plans will fall through and they won't have to go out. My father has been drinking. Not a lot, but enough that it's noticeable. He slurs his words slightly and he sways a little when he stands still, as though he is built like a skyscraper, intentionally designed to be loose so the wind can blow against it, pushing it a few degrees without breaking it. This is the state that embarrasses my mother.

Grace has a stomach ache and my mother keeps asking her if she's ok, does she feel like throwing up? Grace says it's more of a cramp and that it's maybe getting a little better, but my mother says she thinks they ought to stay home, it might be her appendix. My father says the appendix is on the other side and to hurry, they're going to be late. It's Uncle Romeo's birthday and the family will be there, as well as some friends from the old neighborhood where he and Uncle Romeo grew up. My father does not want to miss this party. After they have gone, Grace sits up and she seems fine. She's pale, but then she always has a whitish tinge to her face, so it's hard to tell when she's sick. I'm thinking she didn't really want my mother to leave.

Before leaving for the reunion, my father has made popcorn for us. "You girls need popcorn!" he'd announced. "Can't watch TV on a Saturday night without popcorn!" He's made too much, he used the lobster cooker and we have enough to last days. But we don't say that, we don't joke about how he must think we are his own private army, we just say thank you and I fill a large bowl for Grace and me to share. My mother doesn't say we aren't allowed to eat on the couch, which is what she'd normally say, but she does manage to pass me a warning look.

We watch a movie and finish off the entire bowl of popcorn, then Grace really does get sick. She races upstairs and throws up. I start to worry about appendicitis, I have no idea what the symptoms are and whether vomiting is a sign of it. I wish my mother had not mentioned the word *appendix*, because after Grace throws up a third time, she is convinced she felt her appendix burst and she is dying. I tell her she's fine but still she wants me to stay with her so I sit down at the end of her bed and tell her I'll stay there until she falls asleep.

But a dying child doesn't fall asleep. She talks. She talks about everything she can think of, worried that every story she tells, every memory, is the last one she will get the chance to recount. There is still so much more to say before her appendix finally kills her. She gets tired, but she keeps talking, her words muddled into nonsense as she becomes more asleep than awake, and it sounds to me like she is talking about a dream she is living through even as she speaks.

Whenever I try to get up, she jerks awake and tells me to stay, that she still feels scared. I tell her she's fine, that I have to clean up downstairs and shut the television off. That I'm tired and I want to go to bed, too. "You can call me," I tell her, "I'll be right downstairs and I'll shut off the TV so I'll be able to hear you." But she won't let me go and so I continue to sit at the end of her bed, staring at the alarm clock. It needs a new battery, I remember. It is stuck on four o'clock, stuck there for weeks now and so I have no idea what time it is when I hear my parents come home. All I know is that it's late and I'm tired.

But when I hear my father's voice, I am wide awake. I know what voice that is. It is the voice I hear when he is angry. The drunk kind of angry that we spend our lives trying to head off. But once it starts, we are powerless to stop it. It's like a wave that started half way across the world and has been charging toward our shore, increasing in speed and power.

When this wave rises toward us, we come to realize how weak we are, that we could be made of sand. I feel this weakness in my arms and legs as I walk down the stairs. My legs can barely hold me and if I were to fall, my arms wouldn't be able to clutch the banister.

I sneak into the living room and pick up the popcorn bowl. There are kernels in the bottom of it and it is greasy with too much butter. I think about hiding it, running back upstairs and getting into bed and pretending to be asleep, but my father storms into the living room and stops dead when he sees me.

We stare at each other for a moment, I am holding my breath. He is taking a breath. "What have I told you about cleaning up after yourself?"

he screams. "I do not want to walk into a filthy house. This is my house. I pay for it, and I expect you to keep it clean!" The force of his words is a tempest, fierce and wet with spit that flies from his mouth as he yells. I raise my arms up in front of my face as he reaches for me. He grabs my arm and drags me into the kitchen, where my mother is standing, frantically emptying the popcorn into the trash can. He pushes her back against the wall and tells her to leave it alone, that I need to clean it. That I need to learn. My mother's face is wretched as she holds out the half empty lobster pot and I want to tell her not to worry, but my voice is lost. I empty the pot and start filling it with hot water and soap and I place the bowl into it so I can wash it. But I haven't emptied out the kernels of corn that are stuck to the bottom of the pot and my father pushes me away from the sink, pulls the bowl out of the soapy water and shakes it in front of my face, telling me that the kernels will get stuck in the drain and that he'll have to call a plumber to clean it out and was I prepared to pay for it? I stand there and do nothing.

"Take this bowl and clean it right!" he says, his voice is seething with anger and he shoves the bowl in my face and I have to turn away so I don't get soap in my eyes. He presses the bowl into the side of my head and says, "Do you understand me?" in a slow voice, like I am retarded and he has to take great care to make sure I know what he expects of me. I take it from him but I am so confused, so scared, that I immediately forget to empty the bowl into the trash and I drop it back into the lobster pot that is now overflowing with hot water.

And then the full force of the wave hits the shore. "What did I just say?" he screams. "What did I just say?" He grabs me by the wrist and flings me across the kitchen, but he doesn't let go of me and I hear a snap and then my mother screams. A pain, like a metal spike, shoots up my arm and I feel light headed. I drop to my knees and close my eyes against the bright stars that have appeared in front of me.

"You broke her arm, you broke her arm!" My mother is shrieking these words over and over and doesn't stop until he hits her. She falls against the wall and sinks to her knees. Through the light that is still popping in front of my face, I can see that she is holding a hand over her mouth. In a voice that is now calm, my father says, "Well, I guess I'll clean up this mess all by myself, since it seems I can't get any help from the two of

you."

It is the drunk in him that allows him to weave around us as he wash-
es the bowl and the lobster pot, wipes them dry and puts them away. He
says good night as he stumbles out of the kitchen and I can hear his body
knock into the furniture and the walls as he makes his way upstairs.

After he leaves the kitchen, my mother gets slowly to her feet. Her
mouth is bleeding and she wipes it with the back of her hand, leaving a
streak of red. She kneels down next to me and checks my arm. She touch-
es it and I scream. She stands and looks at me. There is something about
her that is hesitant. She stares at my arm and doesn't move. After a minute, she walks out of the kitchen. When she returns, she is holding her
purse in one hand and the car keys in the other. She asks me if I can
stand, if I can walk to the car. She says she has to take me to the emer-
gency room.

CHAPTER Fourteen

In the morning light, I could see my mother's face was bruised. A flying plate or mug, maybe a flying saucer, had caught her under the eye. She had what looked like a dark blue ink stain under her left eye that spread to the top of her cheekbone. The sun came in through the picture window and lit the features of her face and I wondered what else had hit her, what other bruises were hidden under the hand-crocheted afghan she had wrapped herself in.

I woke up tangled in the sheet that my mother had tucked so tightly under the mattress. It scared me at first, even though I knew, instinctively, I wasn't trapped. It was just a white sheet, so thin and worn I could see my hand through it. I sat on the edge of the pullout couch and watched my mother sleeping. She stirred and slid around on the slick leather of the chair and then jerked awake. She shielded her face from the light with both her hands, like a reluctant actor caught in the spotlight, unrehearsed.

I got up before she woke all the way, slipping off the creaking bed as quietly and quickly as I could. It was still fairly early, but Mr. Bergeron had already left for work. I knew he had gone down to the shipyard, he and Mrs. Bergeron had talked about it the night before, as Mrs. Bergeron was hemming us into the bed, telling us to get a good night's sleep and shutting off the light. He had promised that he wouldn't do much, that he'd just stand around and do what he did best, which was to tell other people what to do. He had promised he wouldn't use his hand. Mrs. Bergeron was in the kitchen by herself, reading the paper and drinking coffee. She looked up as I came in.

"Morning Claire," she said. "You sleep good?" She did her best to make me feel like I belonged there, like I were a planned guest instead of a refugee. "Coffee's ready if you want to bring your mother some."

"Thanks," I said. I opened one of the cupboards and took down a cup. The coffee had been on the stove for a while, so it had reached a dark brown color, like burnt sugar, and had a honey-like consistency. I knew, at this stage, it would need a lot of milk. Before I could bring it to her, my mother came into the kitchen. She had the afghan clutched around her shoulders even though the day was already beginning to warm up. I put the coffee on the table and she sat down. The Bergeron's kitchen table was white Formica scattered with gold dots and rimmed with stainless steel. The chairs were composed of steel legs, the seat and backs encased in glossy vinyl, red as chokecherries. It made their kitchen look a little like a diner. It was cheery, and we sat there, unequal to the demands the furniture made on us.

My mother picked up the cup of coffee and took a hesitant sip, testing it to see how hot it was. "I don't know what to do." My mother's voice was as dull and listless as her expression. "I don't know how long this can go on." She sipped at her coffee, and the color started coming back to her face. "You make the best coffee Jeannette. I don't know how you do it."

Mrs. Bergeron latched onto the coffee theme. When it came to my father, she didn't like to get involved, not when he was drinking.

"You need to get yourself a percolator, that's what. Those fancy coffee makers don't know what they're doing," she said. My mother nodded her head in agreement, trying to grasp onto some topic of conversation that could free her mind, at least briefly, from thoughts of the night before. The flying saucers and other violence that should rightly not belong to this world. I knew this was going to be a half-hearted conversation at best, and one I wouldn't be taking part in. They could talk about coffee pots versus percolators without me. I needed to go somewhere else. I left through the kitchen door without saying anything because I didn't want to invite any kind of conversation. I held onto the handle as I shut the door so as not to let it slam. I didn't want Mrs. Bergeron to throw her coffee cup, since my mother was already at the end of her rope.

There was a small patch of trees that separated our neighborhood from the high school. It wasn't large enough to be called a forest, but it was still fairly dense. At some point in the school's history, it had been dubbed The Gathering because it was such a strange congregation of pines, birches and oak trees. The expansive arms of the oaks reaching around the smaller trees, as though gathering them together in a private huddle. During the school year, it was a popular place for kids to hang out whenever they decided to skip school, but in the summer it was pretty much deserted during the day, and only occasionally used by kids at night. Sometimes we could see the flicker of a small fire through the trees, and the distant glow of cigarettes like dancing fireflies. I went to this little gathering of trees that morning, cutting behind of few of the neighbors' yards.

I followed the slightly worn path to the base of a soaring oak tree that stood at the very center. This was the gathering place within The Gathering, complete with a small fire pit dug into the ground and large rocks that had been rolled into a semi-circle around the blackened hole, the rocks placed flattest side up to you could sit on them, though not very comfortably. There were beer bottles and cigarette butts scattered everywhere and I wondered about these kids who came here. Why, I wondered, do people go to the trouble to create a nice place to hang out, only to fill it up with garbage? I kicked the bottles out of the way, and used a pine bough like a broom to scrape cigarette butts and empty cigarette packages into the fire hole. I covered the hole with a layer of pine needles. The next time a bunch of high school kids came out here, they could burn it all at once, the trash and pine needles together in one single blaze.

When I had finished cleaning up, I sat down on one of the rocks. It was cold and maybe a little bit damp from the night air that hadn't evaporated yet. I contemplated going back to the Bergeron's house to grab a blanket so I could sit on it, but I knew I was just wasting time. I needed to sit. Just sit and figure out what to do. I was at a crossroads. I had read about these types of things, a point in life when you have more than once choice, but I had never really cared. I'd always had a vague notion that fate was untouchable.

I could stop. I could stop looking for signs of my father's binges, stop looking for hidden bottles and pouring them out as I found them. I could continue the duck and cover routine the way I'd always done and just get through it, the way my mother did. I could do nothing.

Or I could continue. I could keep cutting the wires. I had one more play to make, I still had the antabuse tablets. I wasn't quite sure what they were or how they worked, but I knew that when my father took a pill every day, he didn't drink. It was supposed to make him sick because the pills didn't mix with alcohol. I could grind them up, smash them with a hammer the way I smashed peppercorns for our famous marinade, and pour the pills, now a grainy white powder, into a bottle of scotch. They'd swirl around like glitter in a snow globe, but he wouldn't see them because he'd be blind drunk.

"What are you doing here so early?" Celeste popped up behind me with the suddenness of a jack-in-the-box flying out of his little prison. I hadn't heard her coming through the woods, which was surprising since Celeste wasn't known for her stealth.

I twirled around on my seat. "How'd you even know I was here?" I asked her. "You scared me half to death, by the way. Thanks."

"You're welcome," she said. She looked around the clearing, kicked at a few stray cigarette butts. "I saw you sneak across the Gerard's yard. We haven't been here in a while. Remember we used to come here all the time in summer? It's kind of cold." She rubbed her arms and danced around on her toes.

"I know," I said, "I should have brought a sweatshirt. There's no sun here."

"Gosh, I haven't been here in so long, why don't we come here anymore?"

"Cuz it's cold and filthy. It's a lot worse than it used to be. You should've seen how many cigarette butts there were. I swept up about a thousand. And it smells like old beer."

"Remember that time you got in big trouble? That time you tried to miss your piano recital?" Celeste was laughing the way she did whenever she remembered a good joke. I didn't remember it being so funny.

It had been a few summers ago. I'd gone into The Gathering to get away from the house. I was supposed to be in a piano recital that afternoon and I was attempting to avoid it. I wasn't a recital type of person, but my parents thought the event was going to immortalize me and they couldn't wait. My father was even planning on taking the tape recorder with him, despite the fact that I played piano like a six year old. And I was twelve. About a half hour before we were supposed to leave, I went out to the woods with a book and a bag of chips. I sat down on the ground and leaned against the trunk of a pine tree that had fallen over ages earlier, probably before I was born. The bark had been eaten away over the years, just smooth wood remained, and the tree was fairly comfortable to lean against. It was quiet and I got quite a bit of reading in before I thought it was safe to head back. I was a little nervous, since I was pretty sure I'd be in trouble for 'losing track of time' and missing the recital. But at that moment, I thought it was worth it. I'd take punishment over public humiliation any day.

As I stepped out of the darkness of the trees and across the Gerard's backyard, it seemed like a lot of neighbors were outside, more than usual for a Saturday afternoon, and they all seemed to be talking at once. I was ambling down the street as though I was just enjoying the day, when a police car slowly passed me and stopped at the foot of my driveway, where the whole neighborhood had converged. The car was silent, but the lights flashed a dark blue light and even though it was bright outside, the light was visible, a perverse shining darkness. I was suddenly afraid something had happened to Grace, and so I ran.

It's funny how anxiety and fear can make people blind. Grace was standing perfectly still in the midst of the crowd, unsteady on her feet and though she looked right at me, I could tell I was invisible to her. My father was pacing back and forth, nodding repeatedly in the direction of Mr. Gerard who was yelling at the top of his lungs, trying to get everyone organized into a search party.

My mother was crying, saying "Where could she be?" over and over, like a broken record that needed to be thrown out. I stood there a full two or three minutes before anyone noticed me. When they finally did, my parents stood there for a while, and I could almost see the mechanics of their brains working to grasp that I was right there in front of them. There were two police officers, a short stubby one who stood next to my mother, holding her arm like he was afraid she might fly off somehow. The other police officer came up to me and asked, "Is this the young lady?" The crowd, now silent, nodded in unison. The officer asked me if I was ok.

I nodded.

He asked me again if I was all right and whether I had been gone of my own accord and he stood there, silent, waiting for an answer.

But my heart, lungs, everything, had already dropped into the pit of my stomach and I couldn't do more than just stand there. I finally managed to say 'oops' or something stupid that made the entire neighborhood believe that I didn't take the situation seriously. The police officer, an unusually tall man, looked down at me for a few seconds before turning in my mother's direction and tipping his hat toward her and nodding to his partner that they could go. If this had been a lighter situation, say like the time Mr. Bergeron called the police to report his car stolen only to have Mrs. Bergeron drive up in it as he was filling out the police report, my father and I might have gotten a kick out of the Laurel and Hardy act. But I didn't dare make eye contact with him. The tall and short officers got back into their patrol car and rolled down the street as silently as they had driven up it, but now with the lights off.

I was grounded for the rest of the summer, I wasn't allowed to leave the neighborhood, and The Gathering was off limits indefinitely. From that summer on, the innocent little copse came to represent something threatening, and even though I'd grown up some since that summer, I found that the feel of the place had changed permanently. It somehow wasn't fun or cool to sneak into anymore. Now I had to walk through threads of guilt, like a spider's web, to get there.

"Remember what that cop said about your mother when they left? The short, fat one?" In a deep yet effeminate voice, she mocked him. "That lady will never be the same!" Celeste snorted a little as she sat down. It was true, we had found some humor in the situation, eventually. We could usually find some element of hilarity in anything. From then on, every time we witnessed someone in a state of panic, even if it was a man, we'd look at each other and say, "That lady will never be the same!"

I wondered what Celeste would think at that moment if she'd known about the frenzied fighting at my house that night. I knew that when she saw my mother's face that morning, she'd think those words to herself, 'that lady will never be the same!', but she wouldn't say them out loud. And the words, as they danced around in her head, would make her heartsick. Words are slippery, unmanageable things. Weak and shapeless, stealing meaning from the situations that create them. I didn't say anything right then to Celeste about what had happened, or that we'd had to spend the night at the Bergeron's. I didn't have to, she'd figure it out pretty easily. So she'd ask her mother if I could stay over that night at her house, and she'd have a desperation in her voice that even her mother could understand. And neither one of them would say anything to me because words always come out wrong.

We left The Gathering. Even as I stepped out of the shadows of the trees and into the sunlight, I still felt cold. I told Celeste I had to go to the Bergeron's to get my sweatshirt. She hesitated one second before she said ok, she'd go with me. She asked me if Mrs. Bergeron had made cinnamon rolls and then, just like I knew she would, she asked if I wanted to spend the night at her house.

CHAPTER Fifteen

M rs. Bergeron was, in fact, making cinnamon rolls. She and Grace were kneading a huge pile of dough on the formica table, which was heavily dusted with flour. Small clouds of flour dust hovered over their hands as they pushed the dough down, and folded it over on itself, and pushed down again.

"Grace, you try it on your own now, let's see how you do." Grace looked momentarily terrorized as she was handed this enormous responsibility, but when Mrs. Bergeron said to go ahead, there was no real way to ruin dough anyway, she started pounding. My mother was still sitting at the table, her hands resting on a half-filled cup of coffee, probably the same one I had fixed for her. When Mrs. Bergeron stood next to her and poured her more coffee, my mother started like she'd been asleep with her eyes open.

"I've got to go," she said. "I've got to get ready for work." She got up and headed for the door. Mrs. Bergeron peeled the afghan off her shoulders before she stepped outside. "It will be all right," Mrs. Bergeron said to her in a low voice. "I'll look after Grace today." My mother thanked her, then she said, "And thank Emile for me. I don't know what we'd do without him."

It was right around then I caught a glimpse of myself in the side of Mrs. Bergeron's toaster. "What in the world am I wearing?" I asked out loud. "What the heck!"

"I was wondering what you had on," Celeste said. "I didn't want to say anything."

I looked like I was auditioning for a circus. Why I even owned a pair of plaid shorts, I'll never know, but I did, and I had matched them with a paisley shirt.

Celeste did her snort laugh. "It looks like you got dressed in the dark."

For a moment, just a short second of time, Grace stopped beating the dough before folding it over on itself and continuing her pattern of hitting, stretching and folding, over and over, waiting for Mrs. Bergeron to tell her to stop, it was enough.

"I could change, I guess."

"Please do." Celeste was picking at the dough and Grace slapped her hand out of the way.

I wasn't nervous about going back in the house. My father would be unconscious at this hour since his drinking binges turned him into a vampire. I heard the shower running when I opened the door and figured my mother would probably be getting ready for work. This would have been the perfect time to crush the antabuse tablets and mix them into the scotch bottle that I knew was in the old bureau downstairs. He was past the point of trying to hide it. I could have done it. I even went so far as to run upstairs and pull the envelope with the pills in it out of my dresser. I held the white envelope in my hands, feeling the bulge of the tablets through the paper with my fingers. But I put the envelope back and slid the drawer shut. I changed my clothes, throwing the shorts in the back of the closet so I wouldn't reach for them again. I wasn't too fond of that shirt either, so I shoved it underneath all my other shirts.

I don't know why I gave up. Why, for no clear reason, I decided I wasn't going to do it. Maybe it was because my mother came into the room when I held the envelope in my fingers and when I looked at her as she stood in my doorway, I noticed the bruise on her cheek. The darkness of it made me touch my own face and I felt a sudden pain that throbbed in time with the pulse of blood behind my eyes. Maybe it was because I wouldn't have had enough time, that my mother would be ready to leave for work before I could find the hammer. Maybe I was afraid he'd wake up and find me kneeling in front of his hiding place and I would be trapped down there with him.

And that was the actual truth, if I would tell the truth. I was afraid. I felt clawed inside. Whatever I wanted to convince myself of, I knew down in my shredded soul that I did not dare go down to the cellar and pour crushed medicine in my father's alcohol. I did not dare make him sick. Sicker and angrier.

"Are you ready to go Claire?" My mother was still standing in the doorway, and she watched me as I put the white envelope back in my dresser drawer. She was wearing a bathrobe and her hair was dripping. "I don't want you to stay here today. I want you to stay out of the house."

"I know Mom," I told her. "I'm going. Can I stay at Celeste's tonight?"

"Sure," she said lightly, as though there was no particular reason I was asking. But then she hesitated, looked past me and stared out the window for a moment. She could have been looking at the trees that stood tall and green in the backyard, or she could have been trying to see past them and they were only blocking her view. "And, um, if you can, see if there's someplace Grace can spend the night. She doesn't like to stay at the Bergeron's without you. And don't forget to brush your hair before you leave."

I told her ok, I'd figure something out. I went into the bathroom as my mother opened the door to her bedroom, both of us slinking smoothly through the doorways, like ghosts, as silent and invisible as we could make ourselves. I brushed my hair, decided it didn't look too dirty, and brushed my teeth. I took mine and Grace's toothbrushes with me and wondered at how simple it was to leave the house. With just a toothbrush, I could leave the place where I slept and ate, the rooms that seemed alive when I was in them. I could leave them darkened and emptied and live somewhere else until whatever storm was brewing had passed. It was better this way, I thought. Better to simply walk out the door, do my living somewhere else until the house was my own again, rather than interfere with the enemy. I would retreat and gain ground another time.

I sat on the couch until my mother was ready to leave. I couldn't leave her in the house alone. She came down the stairs in a fitted black skirt with a white blouse. She had smeared make up on her face and it made her look unnatural, not like my mother at all. The bruise was still faintly visible beneath the foundation she had spread under her eye like a cosmetic skin. The lipstick and mascara were probably meant to detract from the darkness that spread above her cheekbone but it only made me kind of sad to look at her.

"Be good today," she said as she got in the car. She didn't give me her usual long list of chores. You'd think that would be a bright side to the situation, but that made me a little sad as well. It's so strange, the way we love the things we hate. She turned the key in the ignition but before she backed down the driveway, she got out of the car and walked over to me. She hugged me tightly around my shoulders. Neither one of us said anything. I noticed she had flesh colored foundation on the collar of her blouse. I rubbed the side of my face after she had left. I was sure I had a light brown smudge of make up on my cheek, same as her blouse

When I got back to the Bergeron's house, I gave Grace her toothbrush and told her to go brush her teeth. The dough for the cinnamon rolls was in a glass bowl on the counter. Mrs. Bergeron had placed it in a rectangle of sunlight that came in through the kitchen window. She was explaining to Celeste that dough had to rise before it was usable.

"The best cinnamon rolls don't come out of a tube, you know." If this was a mild insult tossed in the direction of her mother, Celeste did not pick up on it.

"I know it, but my God, this is going to take forever," she complained. "They won't be ready till lunch."

"It won't go any faster if you stare at it," Mrs. Bergeron told her. "Why don't you go stare at something else, like the television, until they're ready."

Since weekday morning television consisted of Captain Kangaroo and Romper Room, we opted to go outside. Grace stayed behind with Mrs. Bergeron. She had started the whole cinnamon roll endeavor and she felt pretty strongly about seeing it through. That light feeling I had felt before going over to my house was back. Giving up on the Antabuse scheme cleared the dark fog that had surrounded me, the way waking up from a bad dream disperses the evil that haunts you all night long. It was a slow draining, but I could feel it disappearing and I was glad for it.

"What do you want to do?" Celeste asked me. We stood at the end of the driveway and gazed down the street, watching the cars on Main Street pass by, feeling like the whole world was open to us. It was still too early for other kids to be outside. They'd all be in, sitting at their own kitchen tables still, eating corn flakes and watching television for as long as they could get away with it. They'd avoid eye contact, but eventually their mothers would notice they were still in pajamas and tell them to get a move on and go outside.

"We could walk into town," I suggested. "How much money do you have? We could get a donut at Frosty's."

"I've got two bucks," she said, pulling two dollar bills out of her shorts pocket as though she needed to prove it to me.

"That would kill some time," I said.

The chickadees were calling to each other in their high pitched whistles as we headed down the street. I never heard them during the day and I don't know if it's because they were quiet then, or whether the sounds of the neighborhood, as it came to life, drowned them out. We took a right hand turn when we got to Celeste's house and started walking down Main Street.

An enormous white church marked the beginning of the town. Since it wasn't the Catholic Church, we didn't know what denomination it was. It was known simply as the big white church. The end of town was cut off by the river. In between was one long street that held pretty much everything we'd ever need. Our habit was to walk down one side, cross the street at the river, in front of the bridge, and walk back up the other side. Without needing to talk about it, we crossed over when we reached the church so that our first stop would be Sherman's Fruit Co., which never sold any fruit for at least as long as I was alive. But they did sell candy, so we used one of Celeste's dollars to stock up.

As we chewed gum and sucked on candy necklaces, we meandered slowly down the wide sidewalk, stopping briefly at storefronts to look inside and imagine what we'd buy if we had the means. Or the need. Outside the furniture store, Celeste pointed to a pure white couch and said she'd have an all-white living room when she had her own house. "It's going to be cool," she said, "white walls, white shag carpet. I might even do white drapes."

"Everything will be pretty much invisible Celeste." I imagined her room, all white and mysterious shadows, like a room of snowdrifts.

"I know," she said. "That's what will be so cool about it."

We passed the deli next and stood outside to read the menu, which never changed. It left us starving for a Rueben, but we didn't have enough money. The deli never opened before lunch anyway.

The next building was the book store. We usually didn't do more than look in the window of this place, just curious to see if anyone we knew was inside. I used to love this bookstore. There were couches all over the place and the owners would let you read whatever you wanted, even the little kids. I could spend hours in there when I was a kid, reading one mystery after the other, never embarrassed that I read more than I purchased. But now it only reminded us that school was days away, and we hurried past.

Our next stop was the paper and office supply company, where my mother worked.

"Oooh, let's get some paper!" Celeste yelled, bounding up the granite steps. For some reason, she was obsessed with paper. I don't know what she did with it, I never saw her write anything, never saw her make so much as a paper airplane. Her whole house had to be a fire hazard by now. But every time we walked downtown, she had to go in the paper store. A bell chimed from somewhere overhead and my mother stood up from behind a desk where she had been sorting papers. "Can I help you?" she asked us, her voice sweet and quick, like she was singing rather than talking. When she saw, she said, "Oh, it's you two. Where's your sister?"

"She's still at the Bergeron's," I told her, "she didn't want Mrs. Bergeron to finish the cinnamon rolls without her."

Celeste had said good morning to my mother and walked to the back of the store where they kept the paper, big stacks of it piled on shelves that ran all along the back wall. I guess if you liked paper, it was paper heaven. Reams of the stuff were set up like a rainbow, the reds way over on the left, softly changing into the next color until ending in the deep blues. You could buy colored paper by the sheet back then, and my mother let Celeste take one sheet of colored paper from each stack. It was a lot of paper, at least twenty sheets, and she had trouble carrying them around. They kept sliding out of her grasp and my mother had to give her a bag.

I was more interested in the pens, but my mother never let me take one. I suppose if she had let me take something for free, it would have been a little like stealing. We poked around the store for a while and ate half my mother's lunch before real customers came in and she shooed us out.

We jumped down the granite steps back onto the sidewalk and raced each other to Frosty's Donut Shoppe. If you wanted a real donut, this is where you went. It was A Man's Donut, as the slogan proclaimed, and they really were about as big as your head. Celeste paid, dropping the last of her money into the tip jar, which she did whenever a high school student was working. She thought it might possibly help her out once school started. The donuts were still warm. The cracked glaze clung to our cheeks and chins the way the right kind of snow sticks to tree branches. We brushed it off with our hands since neither of us had remembered to grab napkins.

From there, it was only a short walk to the river. We stepped over the guardrail. There were deep dents all along it and I always wondered how many cars may have careened over the edge and into the rushing water but for someone else's vigilance. We sat down, our backs to Main Street, and looked out across the river.

The Androscoggin flowed fast here, and there were always white caps that dotted the top of the water, except they were yellow. That's what a century of waste gets you - a big long cesspool. Our old textile mill sat, worn and broken, on the other side of the bridge, it's days of dumping toxins into the river over for decades. It was hard to imagine this river had been even more disgusting. According to my father, the water used to be brown and covered in a thick, waxy foam. He knew someone who drowned when he was a kid, some boy who thought the river was solid enough to walk on. But the mills were shut down, and the river was on a mission to clean itself. If people left it alone it could, in time, revert back to its original state. A rebirth, of sorts. But for now, it was still an unnatural color and gave off a sickly odor, the kind of smell so heavy and rich that if you breathed it in too long, you'd feel as though you'd eaten it.

We watched the river in silence for a while. It had a mesmerizing effect on us. But then the smell began to settle around us, and I threw the rest of my donut as far as I could, missing the water by several yards. I'd always had a weak arm.

"How can you eat with that smell?" I wiped my face with my arm since my hands were thoroughly sticky by this point.

"I can take it," she said, stuffing the last of her donut in her mouth.

"This smell kind of makes me want to puke. Let's head back."

The walk back was not as fun. The other side of the street was also not as interesting. There was an insurance company, a real estate agency, and an old lady clothing store. We went in there once and tried on a bunch of clothing, a lot of silky lavender dresses with heavy beads threaded into them. We lasted about half an hour before the sales lady kicked us out and told us we weren't allowed back without our mothers. As we passed the store, we both smiled at the memory of it.

When we were about half way up Main Street, two girls, maybe ten years old, stepped out of the doorway of the jewelry store, laughing hysterically at something. They turned to walk down the sidewalk toward us. The white church loomed above them from its perch at the head of the street, and it looked as though they were caught in a steepled shadow. They each wore a set of candy necklaces and bracelets. At first I thought they were chewing at their wrists, like rats trying to free themselves from a trap. We approached each other slowly and Celeste nodded slightly and said hi. They stared at us for a second and then said, "Hi yourself." They spoke at the same time, two small voices that even together didn't sound like much.

They stood close to each other and made no move to step aside, and so Celeste and I had to break apart and step around them. After we had passed the girls, all four of us turned around and looked at each other again. The two girls broke the gaze first, they put their arms around each other's shoulders and started laughing again, knees bent so it looked like they were going to fall over. Only I didn't think they were laughing at whatever it was that had first started their hysterics. They were laughing at us. Somehow I could tell that. But it didn't bother me, or at least it shouldn't have. Celeste and I would have laughed too, in that situation. We laughed at everything at that age.

I can look back on those girls now, all four of them, and they feel like strangers to me. Or maybe characters in a book who once made an impression on my dreams but who I've now half forgotten. Whoever we are, it is never who we were. We were once those girls, Celeste and I, but by the end of that summer, we would be someone else. Who we were right at that moment, I don't know. But I do know this: we were no longer adorable little girls, even if we walked around town, free as the wind, with candy necklaces hanging like precious stones around our necks.

CHAPTER Sixteen

Girls! It's time for lights out. Both of you need to stop talking and get some sleep!" Mrs. Cartier gave the bedroom door one more loud rap for emphasis. Then we heard her heels clicking away down the hall toward the kitchen, where she was going to top off the one martini she was having. It was late, and I was pretty tired, but I was not ready to give in to the day and fall asleep.

We had walked back home after running into those two little girls downtown. We'd gone straight to Celeste's house and were immediately bored to death. It was late in the morning by now, but the street was still quiet. We laid on her bed, feet up on the wall, heads hanging over the edge, and listened to Terry Jacks sing *Seasons in the Sun* over and over. You'd think we'd get tired of hearing the same sob story over and over, the one about the young man who's dying of cancer and saying good-bye to everyone, making sure they all knew how important they were to him. But it struck it us like a knife, every verse, every time we listened. We had a running contest to see who could last the longest without crying. So far, I was winning since Celeste never lasted more than one verse and I could usually hold out till the end. But neither one of us could sing it through even once. Our voices would break and we'd choke up, trying to laugh through our strangled throats to prove we weren't really serious about this grief.

And then we did a Bobby Goldsboro contest, and that was even worse. *Honey.* What a song. It's the one about the man who's wife dies for no apparent reason, but that's not what was sad about it. It was that he missed her, the whole song was about how much he missed her. If you listened to the words closely enough, you'd realize that he'd kind of made fun of her when she was alive and that she might even have committed suicide because of it, but we didn't care. He was sorry for it now. We could not make it through that song even once, ever. We couldn't even get through the first line. Bobby's child-like voice would beg us to *see the tree, how big it's grown,* and it was all over for the both of us, tears spilling over our foreheads and running in rivulets into our hair because we were still upside down.

Eventually, the songs were drowned out by the loud humming of a naval airplane making a pass over the neighborhood. There were flights that flew right over our heads week after week that we never paid attention to, but since we were in the midst of listening to something else, this intrusion was noticeable. We listened to the deep drone of the engine as it passed us. We had to wait till it was a distance away because it was so loud, we couldn't hear ourselves.

"Listen Claire," Celeste said to me once the air was clear again, "we can't lay around crying all day. Let's see if Grace finished those cinnamon rolls yet."

We rolled off the bed, Celeste's forehead had a slight sheen to it from the tears that had dried and I knew I probably did, too. Celeste's mother was in the living room watching one of her soaps. She had the ironing board out, a basket of laundry on the floor by her feet. The iron was propped up at one end, hissing steam, and her amber glass ashtray was perched at the other end, a lit cigarette sitting atop a pile of its crushed brothers and sisters. She straightened out a handkerchief with the flat of her hand and attacked it with the hot iron. When she saw us, she picked up her cigarette and took a long breath from it. She exhaled like a sick dragon, a lot of smoke with no fire behind it.

"You girls going outside?" Without waiting for an answer, she continued. "Celeste, I want you to set up the sprinkler later for your brothers. I have to go out, keep them occupied, ok?"

"Where are you going?" Celeste asked her.

Mrs. Cartier waited about five seconds before answering. She finally let out a sigh and said, "Did you forget tomorrow is your grandmother's birthday?" She gave Celeste a look. "I'm going to get a little gift, something special for her. I'm leaving right after lunch, so be back here on time."

Mrs. Cartier inhaled another lungful off her cigarette and blew a thin stream of gray smoke at us by way of saying good-bye. She turned back to her ironing and we headed outside.

Celeste griped for a while about how much she hated her grandmother. "She acts like it's her birthday every day! I have to treat her like a queen, no matter what day it is."

Just last year on Grand-Mere Bernier's birthday Celeste was given the honor of making the celebration dinner. It did not go well, primarily because Celeste can't cook, and the Grand-Mere was very clear on how sincerely she did not appreciate her meal. I heard that story every time anyone mentioned the word grandmother or pot roast.

The last time the two of them were together, Grand-Mere told Celeste it was time she started becoming a little more responsible. To help her along, she had a few jobs that needed doing, starting with picking the dead birds out of the car grill. Celeste told her she'd die first, and her grandmother told her she could make that happen.

"Can you believe that?" Celeste yelled, the anger still fresh in her voice like it had just happened yesterday. She relived the event every time she talked about it. Her voice, which got loud when she was angry, rang through the neighborhood. "What kind of a grandmother says that to a child? To her grandchild?"

Celeste was still griping when we reached the Bergeron's house, but she stopped as soon as she threw the door open and caught sight of Grace's creation. The cinnamon rolls were done, huge circles of sweet bread covered with a blanket of icing so thick it looked like one enormous, lumpy cake. And Grace was still pouring it on.

"OK, Grace, you got enough frosting on those yet?" Celeste asked her. She pulled a roll away from the sticky mass and held the dripping roll between two fingers. "This is the kind of thing I live for," she said.

"I accidentally dumped the whole bag of powdered sugar out," Grace explained.

As usual, she hadn't read the directions. Or listened.

"We're calling them Ghost Rolls," Mrs. Bergeron said. Grace kept pouring the viscous white icing over the rolls, turning them into unidentifiable shapes, like ice skates that had been left outside in a storm. They looked good, but I couldn't eat. I was still full from the Man Donut, plus I could still taste the smell of the river. But I promised Grace I would eat one later.

Celeste managed to eat all of hers though. She could be unbelievable at times. Mrs. Bergeron watched us from one corner of the kitchen, her arms folded across her chest, a faint smile on her face. I didn't know what there was to smile at, we were making a mess of her kitchen table. When Celeste was done stuffing herself, Mrs. Bergeron told her to go into the bathroom and wash off.

"Try not to touch the walls," she called after her.

There was a brilliant sunlight coming in through the picture window, I could see signs of life starting up in the neighborhood. From where it stood, the Bergeron's house had a view of the whole street. So this was how Mr. Bergeron always managed to come outside with the Holy Grail of candy bowls at the perfect moment. Just one glance out this window, and he could see us all. I wasn't all that happy as I stood there, where he must have stood countless times, watching the kids race around on bikes, slamming in and out of their houses. It took a little of the mystery away, knowing that he could stand here and count heads, get a sense of how bored we were, what might be a good time to grab the magic candy bowl and go sit outside. He could find that perfect moment when we needed him the most, that moment that would set his popularity at the highest rung.

But I told myself I was fourteen. Time to let it go, maybe time to stop playing outside all the time. The kids that were out, they looked so little, jumping off their stoops like they were Batman when the porch steps were two feet off the ground. Racing around on bicycles like they were in the Indianapolis 500, actually going two miles an hour at top speed. It was all so cute.

"Holy crap," Celeste had come up beside me. She tapped the window pane with her fingernail. "You can see the whole neighborhood from here. Look at those dweebs."

We watched for a while, Celeste slightly bemused while I tried to think of some way to laugh at these kids.

"There's your mother," I said. Mrs. Cartier had come out of her house and was pacing up and down the driveway, I could almost hear her heels clicking as she stalked up and down, glancing now and then at her watch.

"I guess she wants to leave," I said. "We'd better get going."

Grace and I filed out the door behind Celeste, and Mrs. Bergeron told us to have fun. She had a white dish cloth slung over her shoulder and she had put a clean apron on. She looked like a very large Cinderella, smiling at us in that martyred way Cinderella had as she watched the stepsisters trudge out the door, onto bigger and better things.

Celeste's mother started yelling at her before we were halfway down the street. Her voice, stretched thinner than usual, sounded like it would snap from the strain.

"You said get home after lunch," Celeste yelled back, her voice rich and heavy in contrast to her mother, piano chords raised against chicken wire.

"I said before lunch time, young lady."

I was terrified for a second that she was going to ask me to referee this argument, but instead, Mrs. Cartier instructed us to give the boys some lunch and keep them entertained until she got back. She slammed the car door and I wondered why she always had to be so mad. The way she slammed the door, it felt like she was punching us, a loud, hard crack against our skulls.

But Celeste didn't even notice. "Hey guys, I have an idea," she was yelling into the house. Her two little brothers poured out of the front door, stopping at her feet and jumping up and down, hanging on her words like little tiny Tarzans hanging on vines. Even Paul, the serious one, was getting carried away.

"We're going to set the pool up in the backyard, and stick the end of the slide in it."

They started going psycho, a silent sort of insanity where they stared at each other, mouths hanging open, grabbing each other so they wouldn't fall over.

"And...," here she paused for effect. "We're also going to set up the sprinkler!"

That did it. I almost felt sorry for them, the two little brothers. Sometimes such an extreme height of happiness can begin to lose meaning. I mean really, if a makeshift water slide and sprinkler can make someone insane, what happens if something truly good comes along? There is a realm of happiness, and they were at the outer edges of it. A flat earth they might fall from.

"Can we help? Can we help?" they screamed. Without waiting for an answer, they ran to the garage and started jumping at the blue plastic wading pool, which had been hung on a nail just out of their reach. "Get it! Get it!" they yelled. Celeste and I lifted it off the wall and carried it out to the backyard, over to the swing set, and then carefully maneuvered the little pool under the slide. It was made of cheap, thin plastic, and we were afraid to crack it.

"Fill it! Fill it!" they screamed, still jumping. The garden hose was tangled in a giant green ball, and water barely trickled out. I thought they were both going to pass out. But then Celeste got the tangled mass straightened out and they caught their breaths, relieved. They squatted, watching the pool slowly fill, the water clear as glass and freezing cold.

"It's going to take forever if you watch it," Celeste told them. "Why don't you go find the sprinkler head? I think it's in the garage somewhere."

Celeste had already found the sprinkler but this was a good way to keep the boys occupied while we went inside and made lunch. She was always afraid they'd accidentally slip headfirst into five inches of water and drown. "Not on my watch," she'd say, and she'd keep them away from the water unless she was watching them.

Setting up a water park in the Cartier's backyard always triggered a radar effect and we went ahead and made a dozen sandwiches since most of the neighborhood kids would show up within the next few minutes. The three of us worked together with synchronized efficiency, passing each other back and forth between the kitchen counter and the refrigerator. Celeste made bologna sandwiches, Grace made Kool Aid in the biggest Tupperware pitcher she could find and I filled baggies with chips, tying the ends with red and white striped twist ties that for some reason the Cartier's always had on hand. By the time we had all this food set up on the picnic table, the pool was almost over flowing and the kids that had been hanging out at the end of the driveway started marching toward the backyard. We had a "Let the Games Begin" moment as Celeste set the sprinkler up, and then the two of us stood back and watched them all play.

It was a typical gathering, most of the kids having fun, a couple complaining that we hadn't spent an all-nighter filling up water balloons, a few hogging the food. And then, of course, an injury. It never failed. This time it was Benny, the short stocky kid who lived next door to Celeste. He was the type of kid best left ignored. If he got even the slightest bit of attention, he went with it. All it took was some little kid commenting on how his cowboy bathing trunks were cool, and then he was swinging the hose, sprinkler attached, around his head like a lasso. Before Celeste could say, "Shoot, he's going to clock someone," he had clocked Paul in the head.

Foreheads bleed. Profusely. It can be scary, how the blood cascades down the face like a dam has broken. Paul was blind with it. The backyard got immediately still, as blood demands everyone's attention. The only sound was the wet humming of the sprinkler, which continued to rotate back and forth from where it hung off the end of the hose, which Benny was still holding. Water shot gently first toward the left and then slowly to the right, spraying him directly in the face at about the halfway mark.

I didn't know what to do first - grab the sprinkler from Benny before he drowned himself, or put pressure on Paul's head to stop him from bleeding to death. I saw Celeste make a grab for the hose so I grabbed the stack of paper napkins that were on the picnic table and yelled to Celeste to run in the house and get the first aid kit.

"But we don't have a first aid kit!" she yelled back, throwing the sprinkler head into the pool like it was in flames.

"What family doesn't have a first aid kit?" I shouted to her. "Don't you at least have a box of Band-Aids? Check the bathroom for God's sake!"

They did have a box of Band-Aids, miracle of miracles. If there was one family in this neighborhood that didn't have a first aid kit, it would be this one. By the time Celeste handed it to me, I had been pressing a wad of napkins against Paul's forehead. When I pulled it away, I could see the cut, an open red gash against his white forehead. It wasn't bleeding anymore and for a second I thought he had bled to death already. But he was still standing, so I took that as a good sign.

"See if there are any butterfly stitches in there," I said as I handed the box back to Celeste. My hands and fingers were bloody and I didn't want to rifle through the box.

"What the heck are butterfly stitches?" Celeste asked, her voice a nervous twitter.

"Give me anything that doesn't look like a Band-Aid," I told her.

Once, when Grace was learning to walk, she had fallen against the door jamb to our room and split her forehead open, the same red slash I was looking at now. My mother had fallen into her usual hysterics routine, ready to call an ambulance and then the morgue. But my father had told me to hold a cloth against my sister's head and I did. I held it there, applying the right pressure, until he came back. He held small strips in his hands that looked a little like small white butterflies. He squeezed the slit in Grace's forehead together so that it looked like a thin line from a red pencil, and kept it closed with the butterfly stitches. On that hot summer afternoon, I did the same thing to Paul's forehead. It would heal, I knew, into a slim line that would look like someone had scratched him lightly with a pin.

After I closed the hole in his head, I washed Paul's face with more napkins, wetting them with water from the pool.

"Good as new," I told him. "Go have fun. You want a popsicle?"

He stood still for a few seconds, as though he knew he was supposed to carry on like a wounded soldier. He had a right to that kind of behavior, and all the sympathy that went with it. He knew that a gash in the head was like money in the bank, ripe for spending and that somehow he was not getting his money's worth if he started playing. We all hate a missed opportunity.

It took a little begging and I think, ultimately, he did not want to hurt Celeste's feelings. Maybe he thought it would ruin her day. Paul was the sensitive one, the kind of person who takes guilt seriously, like a knife to the heart. Celeste's disappointment would have hurt him more than anything. And so he smiled weakly and walked gingerly across the lawn to the pool, like he had hurt his feet instead of his head. Little kids are like that. They don't mind being hurt, they just want to make sure people know they are suffering.

It worked out for the best. Paul became an instant celebrity on account of his two butterfly stitches and how he barely even cried, and I was a hero for saving him. I think some of the smaller kids actually thought I had saved his life, I could see it in their eyes. Even Mrs. Cartier was impressed when she inspected his head later. She came home very late in the afternoon, almost supper time.

"Thank you Claire," she said to me, "you did a very neat job. I don't even think he needs a trip to the doctor."

We hadn't even noticed how late it had gotten. The kids were all sunburned and the pool was half empty of water and filled with grass. All the food was gone. The day had slunk away unnoticed and evening was seeping in through the trees. And still, the kids were unwilling to leave, everyone wanting that one last minute.

That night, I tried to stay awake. If I could stay awake, the day might never end, I thought. The way little backyard pools never fill if you stare at them. But I couldn't do it, I fell asleep without realizing it, and when we woke the next morning, the day was dark with clouds and the air thick with rain.

CHAPTER Seventeen

I stayed at the Cartier's house as long as I could. The rain kept falling, without giving any sign of letting up and I did not feel like stepping out into it. But Celeste and her family were spending the day with their grandmother. After a series of hints, it became clear that I was expected to head home. Even Paul, with his butterfly stitch still holding his cut forehead closed, asked me when I was going to leave. It was that shock of embarrassment that finally got me moving toward the door.

"I'm sorry," Celeste told me. "I tried to get you to come with us, but my mother said no."

"It's ok," said.

Mrs. Cartier looked impatient. "You want us to drop you at your house?" she asked.

"No," I said, "I can walk."

"No. No, it's raining. Hop in the car, we'll bring you home."

But I wasn't sure where I wanted to go. I wasn't sure where my mother was, whether she had gone to work and left Grace at the Bergeron's again. I didn't want to walk in the Bergeron's house and be the only one there, without Grace. And I didn't want the Cartier's stopping their car in my driveway because then I'd have to go in the house even if I saw that my father was up and walking, Frankenstein-like around the house, stumbling his way to the basement.

"I like the rain," I said. "I've always liked it."

Mrs. Cartier looked at me uncertainly. But ultimately, she didn't care if I chose to walk home in the rain, despite the fact that there is something wretched about walking out into the rain, the steady wet stream that soaks you till your teeth are chattering with cold. Makes you look like you're crying. Nobody likes walking in the rain.

"Suit yourself," she said. "Try to stay dry!" She attempted a smile as she held the door open for me. "Run between the raindrops!"

And I ran. She probably thought I was trying to prove it to her that I could run fast enough to stay dry all the way home. Like I was magic.

Halfway up the street I stopped running. The rain was heavy and hard, and every few seconds a gust of wind pushed against me and I had to lean into it. My hair was dark and my clothes were dripping, water running down my arms and legs. My feet sloshed around in my sneakers. I always hated getting my feet wet. In the end, I didn't really have a choice, I had to go home. I needed dry clothes and I needed a shower.

The house looked abandoned. I didn't see any movement through the windows, no flicker of life. The porch steps cracked under my weight and I held my breath for a moment. There is something about nerves, they seem to be directly connected to a person's sense of hearing. Every move I made sounded like a shotgun blast.

But the noise was only inside my head. No one was up, no one noticed I was home. I went into the kitchen first. I wanted to check whether the cellar door was open or closed. When my father went down into the basement, he shut the door behind him. It was his way of disappearing. The door was open and that meant he was upstairs. The door opened to the inside so closing it meant leaning over the steps to grab the door handle and pull it closed. Even in a stupor, my father knew better than to try that.

I went upstairs and slipped into my bedroom. I sat on my bed, my nerves were unsteady, but only for a moment. This isn't so hard, I thought to myself. My mother and sister were obviously not home, so I'd take a fast shower and then find them at the Bergeron's. Or maybe, since it was so quiet, I could wait downstairs on the couch. I had a book I wanted to finish, I could sit curled up on the couch with a book, like a normal person does on a rainy day. There wasn't any reason my father wouldn't stay asleep. Sometimes you just have to keep breathing and if you only think about that, the coming and going of air, you can live through anything.

In the bathroom, I peeled off my wet clothes while I let the shower run. It took a few minutes for the water to get hot since the furnace was ancient and didn't work any harder than it had to, and the hot water heater was connected to it. The pipes clanged as the water ran, and the furnace started up like an old person, bitter and complaining. But the hot water felt good. It was hard to imagine that one day earlier, the air had been heavy with heat and humidity and the cold water from a garden hose felt good as it sprayed across your skin. And now one day later, I could have stood in a hot shower for hours. But the water didn't stay hot for hours, it seemed it was only a few minutes before I could feel the water lose its heat as the furnace petered out.

I got dressed and untangled my hair with a comb. I was going to brush my teeth, but I had left my toothbrush at Celeste's house so I rinsed my mouth with Listerine and decided I was as clean as I would get. I opened the door and was struck by how the steam from the bathroom thickened when it met the cool air from the hallway. My father was standing there, across the landing, leaning against the wall. The shock of it made me scream, the way you'd scream at a ghost the moment you realized it was real. Only he was a reverse spirit, a solid object in the swirling mist, something you could actually touch if you reached out for it. It wouldn't disappear.

"Hey there Claire!" he said. "I wondered who was in there. Did you have enough hot water?" He smiled. It was a crooked smile, like his face had trouble navigating, the way his arms and legs did, everything about him jerky and uneven as he headed toward the stairs.

"Come on, follow me," he said. "I got a surprise for you!" His voice had that sing-songy lilt to it that I hated. He sounded like a child.

He stood at the top of the landing for a moment and swayed. His arms reached out to either side, waving in the air like a dying bird that is spinning downward and only reluctantly trying to stop, until one hand reached the wall and the other held the banister. Balanced, he slowly got himself downstairs.

"I'm going to make you some lunch!" His words were slurred, but I could understand what he was saying. "One tuna melt coming up! I know that's your favorite."

For me, this was the worst kind of drunk. The kind where he tried so hard to ignore the fact that he'd been drinking steadily for a few days, pretending he was happy and that there was nothing wrong with him. And I think, at these times, he really was happy. When he was like this, he only saw what was in front of him and if it was me, or something else that couldn't cause him any pain, it filled him with the kind of joy a child feels when Christmas lights snap on and fill a dark house with bright light.

"You know Claire," he said. He had stood waiting for me to come down. He didn't speak again until we were in the kitchen because navigating around the living room furniture was hard for him. We made our way to the kitchen like a pair of old people. He told me to take a seat on the stool and pretend I was in a fancy restaurant. He made a big show of getting out the frying pan, trying to twirl it in the air the way he liked to do sometimes, but he dropped it. He picked it up without looking at me, as though dropping the pan was all part of the fun. He turned on the stove and the black coil of the electric stove slowly built to a red glow.

"I was thinking. We should get a dog. A big lab. Maybe a sheepdog, you said you liked those. Some breed that's fun to be around. One that will run with you."

His eyes were sincere. There was a wholesomeness about him to the point where he could have been filming a Wonder Bread commercial. He could see us, Grace and me, running across the lawn with a dog racing along beside us, then running ahead and stopping to wait for us if we fell back too far. He was in his world now, not ours. It was a made-up place that was sometimes dark and sometimes vivid. Right now it was bright, but it would turn dark again soon, night and day falling in a drunken rhythm.

It took longer than it would have normally, but finally he finished grilling my sandwich. It had a little too much mayonnaise, but it was good. Even at his worst, he could still cook. He couldn't count, though. He had only made one sandwich, and from the way he looked at it, I could tell he was hungry.

"Dad, don't you want one?"

"Oh, I don't know," he answered, sitting down and turning around in his chair like he was looking for a waiter. "I'm not too hungry." And then he said, "I guess I could make another one."

He stood up and wavered, but now it looked like he was tired. Just bone tired. "Maybe I'll make a sandwich for myself, too," he mumbled, more to himself than anyone else. He stumbled as he made his way back to the stove. "Should have made them both at the same time," he said, and it still sounded like he was not talking to me. "That's what a smart person would do, make two sandwiches at once."

He was silent while he made his sandwich, scraping the bowl with a spoon to get all the tuna fish out since he had put most of it on mine. I stared at my sandwich, golden brown, melted cheese dripping down the sides like Grace's icing on her cinnamon rolls. If he wasn't drunk, or if he were only a little tipsy, I would have told him about the rolls Grace had made, and how good they were. I would have told him she showed a little promise in the culinary department for the first time ever, but that it was probably due to all the sugar she used. A whole bag! We would have found a way to laugh at her, but all in good fun. She knows we love her, he'd say.

We would have sputtered over our sandwiches as I described the solid mound of icing she had made with Mrs. Bergeron's entire bag of powdered sugar. He would have been impressed with me when I told him how all three of us flew out the door on our sugar rush, and how we made the whole neighborhood happy for a few hours. "You know how to live, Claire. You know how to live. That's a talent, let me tell you." That's what he would have said to me.

But today, because of how he was, we couldn't laugh at anything. So I cried, silent. And he made his sandwich, also silent.

It was still raining when Grace and my mother came home. I had thought my mother had taken Grace to work with her, but she must have taken the day off. She wouldn't have wanted us to be alone. Maybe they came home to get me, but I don't know where we could have gone. We had imposed on the Bergeron's long enough and Celeste was gone. And so we all ended up being home. There was nowhere else for us all to go.

Grace and my mother walked into the house with wet bags of groceries. They had to hold them from the bottom, the way you'd cradle a baby, and set the wet sacks on the counter quickly so they wouldn't tear apart. The brown paper was limp with the rain, I could smell it from where I was sitting.

"What've you got there?" my father asked them. He was too excited again, crossing the kitchen in one long stride and peering into the grocery bags, pulling out the things my mother had bought, one at a time, nodding approval. "This is giving me ideas for a big supper tonight, you just wait!"

For a while, we all tried so hard to be happy. Grace admired my tuna melt like it was something out of National Geographic and my mother thanked him for fixing lunch.

"I worry about Claire sometimes," she said. "Sometimes I think she doesn't eat enough."

She meant it as a compliment. She meant him to understand, even though she was making it up, that she was proud that he could make me something to eat, even if it was only a sandwich, and that it was because he was such a good cook.

"Why?" he asked her. His eyes were changing. His face turning grim. Clown to fiend in a lightning strike. Frightening.

"Don't I feed this family? Isn't that one thing I can do?"

My mother froze. So did her brain. "No, I mean, well, lately I think she hasn't been eating enough. But look at this, this is wonderful." She waved her arm across the dining room table, where my sandwich sat, golden and melted, uneaten.

"She doesn't like how Mrs. Cartier cooks," Grace said. "She actually doesn't like how anyone else in the neighborhood cooks."

She was very matter of fact, sincere even. If anyone asked her, she'd probably have said she was trying to make him feel good. I could see in her eyes that she was trying to turn the ship, make him happy again, the way he had been when she and my mother walked into the house.

"You're a lot better Dad. A lot better cook." Her eyes grew desperate and her breathing started to become shallow as she realized that his face was changing. He was crossing the line into night.

All her life, whenever Grace fell down, stumbled or whatever, we'd say *way to go Grace*. We'd say it if she just did something crazy, like falling down after she twirled around too much. We'd say it even if she fell off her bike, something serious like that, so we could make her forget she had fallen. We got a lot of mileage out of the irony of her name. This quirky, uncoordinated girl.

She doesn't like how Mrs. Cartier cooks.

Way to go Grace.

For a moment my father hung his head and in that moment, I felt so sorry for him I started to cry again. But then the sadness, the shame, the exuberance, it all fell away completely, any kindness inside him disappeared like a magician's most spectacular trick. The kind that leaves you wondering how it was possible that something could vanish while you were staring right at it.

All at once, the pan on the stove started smoking. He had forgotten about his sandwich and the burner was set too high, a bright angry red at having been forgotten. Gray tendrils of smoke swirled like dark dust in the air. My father swore as he turned and grabbed the handle of the pan. He threw it across the kitchen, where it bounced several times in the metal sink until its echo settled into silence. The room was quiet for a moment as my father worked to redirect his sudden anger. He wasn't going to be angry at a pan all afternoon. Grace, my mother, and I stood in the dining room, a few yards from him, the kitchen counter all that was standing in his way. We stood still, like birds on a wire, knowing that whoever moved first was the next target. My mother told us to go outside, and he cocked his head in her direction. She told us again, go outside.

When we were really little and my father would stumble up from the basement, my mother would sometimes send Grace and me into the backyard, to the cover of the trees, and make us wait till she called us in. Our backyard was carpeted with pink clover. At the far end, against the backdrop of the trees, we had thick clusters of knotweed. I would tell Grace that we'd be safe there, that no one could find us in the trees and that if it got late and we missed dinner, we could eat the knotweed and pink clover. The knotweed tasted like rhubarb and the clover was sweet, so sweet they made honey from it. Now, my mother was telling us to go there, to go out in the backyard and stay.

"It's still raining," Grace said.

"Sit under the trees," my mother told us. "It will be all right."

Grace started to cry, her breath caught in her throat. She started to shake, all of her trembling as though just the thought of going outside into the rain was making her shiver with cold.

Now my father faced her, his eyes blinked tightly shut and then open, like maybe he had just woken from a dream and couldn't tell where he was. He asked Grace what she was crying for.

"I don't want to go outside," she told him. Her voice came out wet and thick.

He bent towards her. "Why don't you go to the Bergeron's house, you love it over there so much. Or how 'bout the Cartier's? I hear their house is pretty cozy this time of year."

His voice was lifted into a singing cadence, raw with sarcasm. Precisely the sort of thing Grace couldn't pick up on.

"Nobody's home," she said. There was no mistaking the disappointment in her tone.

He lurched toward her. His foot caught in the stool that sat at the end of the counter, the one I always sat on when I watched him cook, and he almost tripped. He picked it up by the leg and threw it across the dining room. It was heavy and awkward so he couldn't throw it far, but it landed hard on the floor and made the walls shake. In a moment, he was leaning down, his face an inch from my sister's.

"You are an ingrate!" he yelled at her. "A rotten ingrate!"

He took a breath, but before he could unleash anything more against Grace, my mother put herself between them.

"Don't you yell at her," she said, her voice was steely but her hands were shaking.

"I will say what I want to say." His teeth bit against each other as he spoke. "She needs to learn to be grateful for what she has. She turns her back on her family, runs over there, takes what she can from them. Take, take, take. That's all she does. She takes!"

He grabbed my mother by both her arms and lifted her off the floor. He threw her, like he had done with the stool, but she didn't fall. She righted herself and again forced Grace behind her. This time he pulled back his arm and drove his fist into her face. At the last second, as she saw it coming, she turned her head and his fist hit her cheek. There was a sound, and then my mother spun around, falling to her knees. He turned back to Grace, who stood silent and unmoving. Urine ran down her legs and pooled between her feet.

He saw this and prepared a new line of attack. "Are you a baby?" he yelled at her, his face again an inch from her face. "A little baby? Need to use the toilet?"

Her mouth opened in a silent cry as he grabbed her by one arm and pulled her across the living room and up the stairs. All the time, he berated her, the little baby. Up each step he hauled her, her legs moving awkwardly as she tried to climb the stairs behind him so she wouldn't be dragged.

Grace didn't make any noise at all until he lost his hold on her and she fell. And even then, the only noise was from her body - her arms, legs, her head, hitting the steps in quick succession, the sharp beat of a snare drum. Quick and steady until the sound abruptly stopped and she was on the floor at the base of the staircase.

"No. No. Please, no." My mother's voice was low. She got to her feet. I noticed she was limping. My father slid down the stairs, his feet unable to land on the steps properly. If he hadn't been able to hang on to the banister, he would fallen too.

"Grace," he said softly as he leaned over my mother, who was crouched beside Grace. "My Amazing Grace, get up, you're all right."

He tried to reach down so he could pick her up, but my mother was instantly on her feet. Both hands on his chest, she pushed him out of the way. This time, he was the one to falter. He stumbled backwards onto the stairs, sitting down hard. She screamed at him not to touch Grace, screamed at him to get away, to leave us alone. But he did not leave, he sat there silently, until he saw Grace move, saw her crawl onto my mother's lap. They were both crying then, my mother and sister. Such a sad sound the two of them made together.

My father dropped his head. He dropped his head the way he did in church, hands folded on his knees. Silent and waiting.

And what did I do this whole time? I watched. I was unseen, even though I was standing right out in the open. I was not a target this time, Grace was, and that had never happened before. I would like to say that I stood there because of shock and that I tried to move, that I tried to help, but that I just couldn't. It is hard to admit our fright.

Even now, I hate to admit that I did not want to redirect my father's anger toward myself and that I even felt a sense of relief that it wasn't me he had grabbed.

My father did not look at me as he made his way to the basement. He opened the door slowly, and yet it still hit against the wall as it opened. He forgot to turn the light on and so he disappeared into the darkness.

I stood there a little longer, waiting to make sure he was all the way down the stairs so he couldn't reach out grab me, and then I walked to the open door, leaned over the stairs to reach the door knob, and pulled the door closed.

My mother took Grace upstairs and I heard water running in the bathtub. The furnace started up again, sounding even more bitter than before, as though angry that it had to heat up a tank of water a second time. I picked up the stool from the middle of the floor, and set it back in its place at the end of the counter. I sat on it, turned backwards so I could see the cellar door. I sat there, not doing anything but watching the door, though there was plenty for me to do. I could have cleaned the pan that had a molten tuna fish sandwich stuck to it. I could have cleaned the floor where Grace had been standing. I could have opened the kitchen window to let out the burning smell that still clung to the air. I could have called the Bergeron's to see if they were home yet and let them know we might need to come over. But I just stayed on the stool and watched the door. Like it was my mission.

I don't know how long I sat there, I couldn't get a sense of how time was passing. I could hear the water draining from the bath tub and then it was silent upstairs. There was no change in the light outside because of the incessant rain so I couldn't tell from the sun how close it was to evening. But I suppose it doesn't matter what time it was when my father started coming up the stairs. He had been down there long enough to drink his fill, because he stumbled badly as he made his way back up from the cellar. I heard his feet trip, and then what was probably the smacking of his knees against the stairs as he fell.

Finally he was at the door. The knob turned. It turned in one direction and then the other. It seemed he'd forgotten how to open it.

The door rattled against the frame as he pushed hard against it and I was afraid that soon I would hear him pounding. I was afraid that he would be mad at the stubbornness of the cellar door, and that would make him think everything was set stubbornly against him. So I opened the door. I turned the knob, I felt the resistance as he was turning it in the other direction. I pushed the door open, but I don't remember that I pushed it very hard.

I heard him curse, I can't remember now exactly what he said, only that he swore loudly. There was enough light from the kitchen to let me see his face just before he fell, the shock of it as he lost his grip on the door knob. The surprise as he groped for the banister but found only air, nothing strong enough to stop him from keeling over backwards.

CHAPTER Eighteen

The police came. One police car and one ambulance. The sound the sirens made, the two distinct screaming noises combined together, was the first thing I remember hearing. It was all silence up till then, but the sirens ripped open whatever shield was around me and once torn open, the whole world was in my ears.

I was blind, too, in a way. All that was in front of my eyes were flashes of color. The color of my mother, the color of Grace. The color of my father, black in the bag that they took up from the cellar. Blue lights and red lights.

But when the flashing lights faded away, I could see again, the blur of colors shrinking back within the confines of shapes.

A police officer talked to me, he said he had to ask me questions and was I able to answer him. No one else was there, he said. No one else saw what happened. Could I please answer a few questions. I said that was fine. I answered him the best I could, and I think he understood me. He was gray-haired and slightly wrinkled and he looked at me as though he recognized me. I took a moment to answer because I was trying to think whether I had seen him before. But I had only ever dealt with the Abbot and Costello officers. That was years ago. He had to ask me again if I could answer a few questions.

My name is Claire Au Clair. My father named me. He wanted that name so he could make up songs about me that he would call Oh Claire Au Clair and he'd sing them to the tune of Danny Boy.

He named my sister Grace so he could sing songs for her to the tune of Amazing Grace. Yes, that's his guitar.

Yes, he could play it. Sort of.

It rained today. It rained all day. That's why we were all inside.

Yes. My father had been drinking.

I could tell by how he acted. And by how he went down to the cellar. He never goes down there otherwise.

He came up the cellar stairs and he fell. He couldn't open the door, he was trying to push it open when he was supposed to pull it. I opened the door. That's all I did, I opened the door for him.

There isn't more to say, really. School started a few weeks later. I walked around in the   shadow of my father, and no one ever saw me clearly, not for the whole four years I was there. I was someone to fear, a celebrity to stay clear of. Or to be nice to, because she might throw you down the stairs when you least expected, you never knew.

Celeste found out there was more to life than our little street, that no one really cared that her mother wore stilettos to bed and that her father's dentures were too big for his head. She turned into a dancing light.

Grace and my mother grew closer, as though the injuries of that night fused them together as they healed. They would never break completely apart.

Uncle Romeo moved out of his apartment and bought a house. We didn't spend a lot of time there. We really didn't need to leave our house again, but sometimes Grace and I would go over for a slumber party so he wouldn't think buying the house was a complete waste of money. He would tell us stories about our father, mostly about hockey. But sometimes about his cooking and how much he missed it. That the greatest undiscovered irony was how his brother learned to cook in the Army. He'd laugh about that, and then he'd cry a little. Then he'd look at me and tell me he really missed my father's meals, but that he knew it was in my blood and I'd take his place one day.

I missed the Bergerons, especially Mrs. Bergeron. We didn't see as much of them anymore, but we were pretty good at making excuses to see each other. We still had about fifty thousand of their mugs and they had several Tupperware containers that my father had used to send soup and pies over to them. Altogether, it took four years to bring each piece back, since we returned them one at a time, without any efficiency at all.

Willie became a legend. So did my father, in a way. He became a tragic figure, someone who was just too good for this world. They all missed him, the whole neighborhood did. Time scoured the rough edges of his life and he became something of our patron saint. There were always candles lit for him at the church and the sign of the cross always came before any story the neighbors told about him. I didn't let it get to me.

Oh yes, and Uncle Romeo eventually took the tree branch down. He even did it by himself. He managed not to get hurt, though he let it slide off the roof too fast and it took out a piece of the gutter. Eventually, he fixed that too. He fixed everything he could, we all did. At some point, we were as fixed as we were going to get, and so we settled back into a new sort of life. We leave a crooked path, that's something my father used to say, and I think I know what he meant. There are no straight-a-ways, so we can never see where we are going. Just twists and turns we have to follow, but a path nonetheless. We're expected to stumble, even fall. And when we are on our knees, it is not to beg for anything. It is to look at the ground closely, to see where the path is worn so we can stand and start walking again. And we don't give up. We keep following without being lost because in the end we are, all of us, forgiven.

ABOUT THE AUTHOR

Simone Paradis Hanson lives in the Metro-Atlanta area with her husband and three sons. She is originally from Maine which is where all her stories are set, as it is the place she knows and loves the best.

A second novel, *The Disappearance of Rachel Sterling*, will be available in 2017.

Visit her blog at simonehanson.wordpress.com